Emily Sarah Holt

A Forgotten Hero

Emily Sarah Holt

A Forgotten Hero

ISBN/EAN: 9783337188610

Printed in Europe, USA, Canada, Australia, Japan

Cover: Foto ©Andreas Hilbeck / pixelio.de

More available books at **www.hansebooks.com**

A Forgotten Hero

Or

Not for Him

BY

EMILY S. HOLT

AUTHOR OF "MISTRESS MARGERY," "SISTER ROSE," ETC.

" But hush!—what is the utmost that I would?
  To give my life to God is all I could :
  And this may be the way He wills to take,—
  This daily death may be for God's own sake."
                    —ISABELLA FYVIE MAYO.

NEW EDITION

LONDON
JOHN F. SHAW AND CO.
48 PATERNOSTER ROW

ATTRACTIVE GIFT BOOKS.

LONDON: JOHN F. SHAW & CO., 48, PATERNOSTER ROW, E.C.

CONTENTS.

———o———

CHAPTER I.

CHAPTER IX.

CHAPTER X.

CHAPTER XI.

CHAPTER XII.

"They went down the spiral staircase together into the great hall, where three tables were spread. At the highest and smallest, on the dais, were already seated the Queen and the Countess."—*Page* ..

A FORGOTTEN HERO.

CHAPTER I.

CASTLES IN THE AIR.

" O pale, pale face, so sweet and meek, Oriana ! "—TENNYSON.

"IS the linen all put away, Clarice?"

"Aye, Dame."

"And the rosemary not forgotten?"

"I have laid it in the linen, Dame."

"And thy day's task of spinning is done?"

"All done, Dame."

"Good. Then fetch thy sewing and come hither, and I will tell thee somewhat touching the lady whom thou art to serve."

"I humbly thank your Honour." And dropping a low courtesy, the girl left the room, and returned in a minute with her work.

"Thou mayest sit down, Clarice."

Clarice, with another courtesy and a murmur of thanks, took her seat in the recess of the window, where her mother was already sitting. For these two were mother and daughter; a middle-aged, comfortable-looking mother, with a mixture of firmness and good-nature in her face; and a daughter of some sixteen years, rather pale and slender, but active and intelligent in her appearance. Clarice's dark hair was smoothly brushed and turned up in a curl all round her head, being cut sufficiently short for that purpose. Her dress was long and loose, made in what we call the Princess style, with a long train, which she tucked under one arm when she walked. The upper sleeve was of a narrow bell shape, but under it came down tight ones to the wrist, fastened by a row of large round buttons quite up to the elbow. A large apron—which Clarice called a barm-cloth—protected the dress from stain. A fillet of ribbon was bound round her head, but she had no ornaments of any kind. Her mother wore a similar cos·tume, excepting that in her case the fillet round the head was exchanged for a wimple, which was a close hood, covering head and neck, and leaving no part exposed but the face. It was a very comfortable article in cold weather, but an eminently unbecoming one.

These two ladies were the wife and daughter of Sir Gilbert Le Theyn, a knight of Surrey, who held his manor of the Earl of Cornwall; and the date of the day when they thus sat in the window was the 26th of March 1290.

It will strike modern readers as odd if I say that

Clarice and her mother knew very little of each other. She was her father's heir, being an only child; and it was, therefore, considered the more necessary that she should not live at home. It was usual at that time to send all young girls of good family, not to school—there were no schools in those days—but to be brought up under some lady of rank, where they might receive a suitable education, and, on reaching the proper age, have a husband provided for them, the one being just as much a matter of course as the other. The consent of the parents was asked to the matrimonial selection of the mistress, but public opinion required some very strong reason to justify them in withholding it. The only exception to this arrangement was when girls were destined for the cloister, and in that case they received their education in a convent. But there was one person who had absolutely no voice in the matter, and that was the unfortunate girl in question. The very idea of consulting her on any point of it, would have struck a mediæval mother with astonishment and dismay.

Why ladies should have been considered competent in all instances to educate anybody's daughters but their own is a mystery of the Middle Ages. Dame La Theyn had under her care three girls, who were receiving their education at her hands, and she never thought of questioning her own competency to impart it; yet, also without a question, she sent Clarice away from her, first to a neighbouring knight's wife, and now to a Princess, to receive the education which she might just as well have had at home. It was the command of Fashion; and who does not know that Fashion, whether in the thirteenth century or the nineteenth, *must* be obeyed?

Clarice was on the brink of high promotion. By means of a ladder of several steps—a Dame requesting a Baroness, and the Baroness entreating a Countess—the royal lady had been reached at last, whose husband was the suzerain of Sir Gilbert. It made little difference to this lady whether her bower-women were two or ten, provided that the attendance given her was as much as she required; and she readily granted the petition that Clarice La Theyn might be numbered among those young ladies. The Earl of Cornwall was the richest man in England, not excepting the King. It may be added that, at this period, Earl was the highest title known short of the Prince of Wales. The first Duke had not yet been created, while Marquis is a rank of much later date.

Dame La Theyn, though she had some good points, had also one grand failing. She was an inveterate gossip. And it made no difference to her who was her listener, provided a listener could be had. A spicy dish of scandal was her highest delight. She had not the least wish nor intention of doing harm to the person whom she thus discussed. She had not even the slightest notion that she did any. But her bower-maidens knew perfectly well that, if one of them wanted to put the dame in high good-humour before extracting a favour, the best way to do so was to inform her that Mrs. Sheppey had had words with her goodman, or that Dame Rouse considered Joan Stick i' th' Lane [1] no better than she should be.

An innocent request from Clarice, that she might know something about her future mistress, had been to Dame La Theyn a delightful opportunity for a good dish of gossip. Reticence was not in the Dame's nature; and in the thirteenth century—and much later than that—facts which in the nineteenth would be left in concealment, or, at most, only delicately hinted at, were spoken out in the plainest English, even to young girls. The fancy that the Countess of Cornwall might not like her whole life, so far as it was known, laid bare to her new bower-woman was one which never troubled the mind of Dame La Theyn. Privacy, to any person of rank more especially, was an unknown thing in the Middle Ages.

"Thou must know, Clarice," began the Dame, "that of old time, before thou wert born, I was bower-maiden unto my most dear-worthy Lady of Lincoln —that is brother's wife to my gracious Lady of Gloucester, mother unto my Lady of Cornwall, that shall be thy mistress. The Lady of Lincoln, that was mine, is a dame of most high degree, for her father was my Lord of Saluces,[2] in Italy—very nigh a

---

[1] Stykelane and Bakepuce—both most unpleasantly suggestive names —occur on the Fines Roll for 1254.

[2] Saluzzo.

king—and she herself was wont to be called "Queen of Lincoln," being of so high degree. Ah, she gave me many a good gown, for I was twelve years in her service. And a good woman she is, but rarely proud —as it is but like such a princess should be. I mind one super-tunic she gave me, but half worn"—this was said impressively, for a garment only *half* worn was considered a fit gift from one peeress to another —"of blue damask, all set with silver buttons, and broidered with ladies' heads along the border. I gave it for a wedding gift unto ·Dame Rouse when she was wed, and she hath it now, I warrant thee. Well ! her lord's sister, our Lady Maud, was wed to my Lord of Gloucester ; but stay !—there is a tale to tell thee thereabout."

And Dame La Theyn bit off her thread with a complacent face. Nothing suited her better than a tale to tell, unless it were one to hear.

"Well-a-day, there be queer things in this world !"

The Dame paused, as if to give time for Clarice to note that very original sentiment.

"Our Lady Maud was wed to her lord, the good Earl of Gloucester, with but little liking of her side, and yet less on his. Nathless, she made no plaint, but submitted herself, as a good maid should do— for mark thou, Clarice, 'tis the greatest shame that can come to a maiden to set her will against those of her father and mother in wedlock. A good maid —as I trust thou art—should have no will in such matters but that of those whom God hath set over her. And all love-matches end ill, Clarice; take my word for it! Art noting me?"

Clarice meekly responded that the moral lesson had reached her. She did not add whether she meant to profit by it. Probably she had her own ideas on the question, and it is quite possible that they did not entirely correspond with those which her mother was instilling.

"Now look on me, Clarice," pursued Dame La Theyn, earnestly. "When I was a young maid I had foolish fancies like other maidens. Had I been left to order mine own life, I warrant thee I should have wed with one Master Pride, that was page to my good knight my father; and when I wist that my said father had other thoughts for my disposal, I slept of a wet pillow for many a night—aye, that did I. But now that I be come to years of discretion, I do ensure thee that I am right thankful my said father was wiser than I. For this Master Pride was slain at Evesham, when I was of the age of five-and-twenty years, and left behind him not so much as a mark of silver that should have come to me, his widow. It was a good twenty-fold better that I should have wedded with thy father, Sir Gilbert, that hath this good house, and forty acres of land, and spendeth thirty marks by the year and more. Dost thou not see the same?"

No. Clarice heard, but she did not see.

"Well-a-day! Now know, that when my good Lord of Gloucester, that wed with our Lady Maud, was a young lad, being then in wardship unto Sir Hubert, sometime Earl of Kent (whom God pardon!) he strake up a love-match with the Lady Margaret, that was my said Lord of Kent his daughter. And in very deed a good match it should have been, had it been well liked of them that were above them; but the Lord King that then was—the father unto King Edward that now is—rarely misliked the same, and gat them divorced in all haste. It was not meet, as thou mayest well guess, that such matters should be settled apart from his al pleasure. And forthwith, ere further mischief ould ensue, he caused my said Lord of Gloucest to wed with our Lady Maud. But look thou, so obstinate was he, and so set of having his own way, that he scarce ever said so much as 'Good morrow' to the Lady Maud until he knew that the said Lady Margaret was commanded to God. Never do thou be obstinate, Clarice. 'Tis ill enough for a young man, but yet worse for a maid."

"How long time was that, Dame, an' it like you?"

"Far too long," answered Dame La Theyn, somewhat severely. "Three years and more."

Three years and more! Clarice's thoughts went off on a long journey. Three years of disappointed hope and passionate regret, three years of weary waiting for death, on the part of the Lady Margaret! Naturally enough her sympathies were with the girl. And three years, to Clarice, at sixteen, seemed a small lifetime.

"Now, this lady whom thou shalt serve, Clarice," pursued her mother—and Clarice's mind came back to the subject in hand—"she is first-born daughter unto the said Sir Richard de Clare, Lord of Gloucester, and our Lady Maud, of whom I spake. Her name is Margaret, after the damsel that died—a poor compliment, as methinks, to the said Lady Maud; and had I been she, the maid should have been called aught else it liked my baron, but not that."

Ah, but had I been he, thought Clarice, it should have been just that!

"And I have heard," said the Dame, biting off her thread, "that there should of old time be some misliking—what I know not—betwixt the Lady Margaret and her baron; but whether it were some olden love of his part or of hers, or what so, I cast no doubt that she hath long ere this overlived the same, and is now a good and loving lady unto him, as is meet."

Clarice felt disposed to cast very much doubt on this suggestion. She held the old-fashioned idea that a true heart could love but once, and could not forget. Her vivid imagination instantly erected an exquisite castle in the air, wherein the chief part was played by the Lady Margaret's youthful lover—a highly imaginary individual, of the most perfect manners and unparalleled beauty, whom the unfortunate maiden could never forget, though she was forced by her cruel parents to marry the Earl of

B

Cornwall. He, of course, was a monster of ugliness in person, and of everything disagreeable in character, as a man in such circumstances was bound to be.

Poor Clarice ! she had not seen much of the world. Her mental picture of the lady whom she was to serve depicted her as sweet and sorrowful, with a low plaintive voice and dark, starry, pathetic eyes, towards whom the only feelings possible would be loving reverence and sympathy.

"And now, Clarice, I have another thing to say."

"At your pleasure, Dame."

"I think it but meet to tell thee a thing I have heard from thy father—that the Lord Edmund, Earl of Cornwall, thy lady's baron, is one that hath some queer ideas in his head. I know not well what kind they are ; but folk say that he is a strange man and hath strange talk. So do thou mind what thou dost. Alway be reverent to him, as is meet; but suffer him not to talk to thee but in presence of thy lady."

Clarice felt rather frightened—all the more so from the extreme vagueness of the warning.

"And now lap up thy sewing, child, for I see thy father coming in, and we will go down to hall."

A few weeks later three horses stood ready saddled at the door of Sir Gilbert's house. One was laden with luggage; the second was mounted by a manservant; and the third, provided with saddle and pillion, was for Clarice and her father. Sir Gilbert, fully armed, mounted his steed, Clarice was helped up behind him, and with a final farewell to Dame La Theyn, who stood in the doorway, they rode forth on their way to Oakham Castle. Three days' journey brought them to their destination, and they were witnesses of a curious ceremony just as they reached the Castle gate. All over the gate horse-shoes were nailed. A train of visitors were arriving at the Castle, and the trumpeter sounded his horn for entrance.

"Who goes there?" demanded the warder.

"The right noble and puissant Prince Edmund, Earl of Lancaster, Leicester, and Derby; and his most noble lady, Blanche, Queen Dowager of Navarre, Countess of the same, cousins unto my gracious Lord of Cornwall."

"Is this my said noble Lord's first visit unto the lordship of Oakham?" asked the warder, without opening the gate.

"It is."

"Then our gracious Lord, as Lord of the said manor, demands of him one of the shoes of the horse whereon he rides as tribute due from every peer of the realm on his first coming to this lord-ship."

"My right noble and puissant Lord," returned the trumpeter, "denies the said shoe of his horse; but offers in the stead one silver penny, for the purchase of a shoe in lieu thereof."

"My gracious Lord deigns to receive the said silver

penny in lieu of the shoe, and lovingly prays your Lord and Lady to enter his said Castle."

Then the portcullis was drawn up, and the long train filed noisily into the courtyard. This ceremony was observed on the first visit of every peer to Oakham Castle; but the visitor was allowed, if he chose, as in this instance, to redeem the horse-shoe by the payment of money to buy one. The shoes contributed by eminent persons were not unfrequently gilded.

The modest train of Sir Gilbert and Clarice crept quietly in at the end of the royal suite. As he was only a knight, his horse-shoe was not in request. Sir Gilbert told the warder in a few words his name and errand, whereupon that functionary summoned a boy, and desired him to conduct the knight and maiden to Mistress Underdone. Having alighted from the horse, Clarice shook down her riding-gown, and humbly followed Sir Gilbert and the guide into the great hall, which was built like a church, with centre and aisles, up a spiral staircase at one end of it, and into a small room hung with green say.[1] Here they had to wait a while, for every one was too busily employed in the reception of the royal guests to pay attention to such comparatively mean people. At last—when Sir Gilbert had yawned a dozen times, and strummed upon the table about as many, a door at the back of the room was opened, and a portly, comfortable-looking woman came forward to meet

---

[1] A common coarse silk, used both for dress and upholstery.

them. Was this the Countess? thought Clarice, with her heart fluttering. It was extremely unlike her ideal picture.

"Your servant, Sir Gilbert Le Theyn," said the newcomer, in a cheerful, kindly voice. "I am Agatha Underdone, Mistress of the Maids unto my gracious Lady of Cornwall. I bid thee welcome, Clarice—I think that is thy name?"

Clarice acknowledged her name, with a private comforting conviction that Mistress Underdone, at least, would be pleasant enough to live with.

"You will wish, without doubt, to go down to hall, where is good company at this present," pursued the latter, addressing Sir Gilbert. "So, if it please you to take leave of the maiden "——

Sir Gilbert put two fingers on Clarice's head, as she immediately knelt before him. For a father to kiss a daughter was a rare thing at that time, and for the daughter to offer it would have been thought quite disrespectful, and much too familiar.

"Farewell, Clarice," said he. "Be a good maid, be obedient and meek; please thy lady; and may God keep thee, and send thee an husband in good time."

There was nothing more necessary in Sir Gilbert's eyes. Obedience was the one virtue for Clarice to cultivate, and a husband (quality immaterial) was sufficient reward for any amount of virtue.

Clarice saw her father depart without any feeling of regret. He was even a greater stranger to her than her mother. She was a self-contained, lonely-hearted girl, capable of intense love and hero-worship, but never having come across one human being who had attracted those qualities from their nest in her heart.

"Now follow me, Clarice," said Mistress Under-done, "and I will introduce thee to the maidens, thy fellows, of whom there are four beside thee at this time."

Clarice followed, silently, up a further spiral stair-case, and into a larger chamber, where four girls were sitting at work.

"Maidens," said Mistress Underdone, "this is your new fellow, Clarice La Theyn, daughter of Sir Gilbert Le Theyn and Dame Maisenta La Heron. Stand, each in turn, while I tell her your names."

The nearest of the four, a slight, delicate-looking, fair-haired girl, rose at once, gathering her work on her arm.

"Olympias Trusbut, youngest daugher of Sir Robert Trusbut, of the county of Lincoln, and Dame Joan Twentymark," announced Mistress Underdone.

She turned to the next, a short, dark, merry-looking damsel.

"Elaine Criketot, daughter of Sir William Criketot and Dame Alice La Gerunell, of the county of Chester."

The third was tall. stately, and sedate.

"Diana Quappelad, daughter of Sir Walter Quappelad and Dame Beatrice Cotele, of the county of Rutland."

Lastly rose a quiet, gentle-looking girl.

"Roisia de Levinton, daughter of Sir Hubert de Levinton and Dame Maud Ingham, of the county of Surrey."

Clarice's heart went faintly out to the girl from her own county, but she was much too shy to utter a word.

Having introduced the girls to each other, Mistress Underdone left them to get acquainted at their leisure.

"Art thou only just come?" asked Elaine, who was the first to speak.

"Only just come," repeated Clarice, timidly.

"Hast thou seen my Lady?"

"Not yet: I should like to see her."

Elaine's answer was a little half-suppressed laugh, which seemed the concentration of amusement.

"Maids, hear you this? Our new fellow has not seen the Lady. She would like to see her."

A smile was reflected on all four faces. Clarice thought Diana's was slightly satirical; those of the other two were rather pitying.

"Now, what dost thou expect her to be like?" pursued Elaine.

"I may be quite wrong," answered Clarice, in the shy way which she was not one to lose quickly. "I fancied she would be tall"——

"Right there," said Olympias.

" And dark "——

" Oh, no, she is fair."

" And very beautiful, with sorrowful eyes, and a low, mournful voice."

All the girls laughed, Roisia and Olympias gently, Diana scornfully, Elaine with shrill hilarity.

" *Ha, jolife!* " cried the last-named young lady. " Heard one ever the like? Only wait till supper. Then thou shalt see this lovely lady, with the sweet, sorrowful eyes and the soft, low voice. *Pure foy!* I shall die with laughing, Clarice, if thou sayest anything more."

" Hush ! " said Diana, sharply and suddenly ; but Elaine's amusement had too much impetus on it to be stopped all at once. She was sitting with her back to the door, her mirthful laughter ringing through the room, when the door was suddenly flung open, and two ladies appeared behind it. The startled, terrified expression on the faces of Olympias and Roisia warned Clarice that something unpleasant was going to happen. Had Mistress Underdone a superior, between her and the Countess, whom to offend was a very grave affair ? Clarice looked round with much interest and some trepidation at the new comers.

CHAPTER II.

THE MISTS CLEAR AWAY.

" Nec tecum possum vivere, nec sine te."—MARTIAL.

ONE at least of the ladies who had disturbed Elaine's hilarity did not look a person of whom it was necessary to be afraid. She was a matronly woman of middle age, bearing the remains of extreme beauty. She had a good-natured expression, and she rather shrank back, as if she were there on sufferance only. But the other, who came forward into the room, was tall, spare, upright, and angular, with a face which struck Clarice as looking very like verjuice.

"Agatha!" called the latter, sharply; and, laying her hand, not gently, on Elaine's shoulder, she gave her a shake which rapidly reduced her to gravity.

"Ye weary, wretched giglots, what do ye thus laughing and tittering, when I have distinctly forbidden the same?—Agatha!—Know ye not that all ye be miserable sinners, and this lower world a vale of tears?—Agatha!"

"Truly, Cousin Meg," observed the other lady,

now coming forward, " methinks you go far to make
it such."

"Agatha might have more sense," returned her
acetous companion. " I have bidden her forty
times o'er to have these maids well ordered, and
mine house as like to an holy convent as might be
compassed ; and here is she none knows whither—
taking her pleasure, I reckon—and these caitiff hild-
ings making the very walls for to ring with their
wicked foolish laughter!—Agatha! bring me hither
the rod. I will see if a good whipping bring not
down your ill-beseen spirits, mistress ! "

Elaine turned pale, and cast a beseeching glance
at the pleasanter of the ladies.

" Nay, now, Cousin Meg," interposed she, " I pray
you, let not this my first visit to Oakham be linked
with trouble to these young maids. I am well assured you know grey heads cannot be well set on
green shoulders."

"Lady, I am right unwilling to deny any bidding
of yours. But I do desire of you to tell me if it be
not enough to provoke a saint to swear ? "

"What! to hear a young maid laugh, cousin?
Nay, soothly, I would not think so."

Mistress Underdone had entered the room, and,
after dropping a courtesy to each of the ladies,
stood waiting the pleasure of her mistress. Clarice
was slowly coming to the conclusion, with dire dismay, that the sharp-featured, sharp-tongued woman
before her was no other than the Lady Margaret

of Cornwall, her lovely lady with the pathetic eyes.

"Give me the rod, Agatha," said the Countess, sternly.

"Nay, Cousin Meg, I pray you, let Agatha give it to me."

"*You'll* not lay on!" said the Countess, with a contortion of her lips which appeared to do duty for a smile.

"Trust me, I will do the right thing," replied Queen Blanche, taking the rod which Mistress Underdone presented to her on the knee. "Now, Elaine, stand out here."

Elaine, very pale and preternaturally grave, placed herself in the required position.

"Say after me. 'I entreat pardon of my Lady for being so unhappy as to offend her.'"

Elaine faltered out the dictated words.

"Kiss the rod," said the Queen.

She was immediately obeyed.

"Now, Cousin Meg, for my sake, I pray you, let that suffice."

"Well, Lady, for *your* sake," responded the Countess, with apparent reluctance, looking rather like a kite from whose talons the Queen had extracted a sparrow intended for its dinner.

"Sit you in this chamber, Cousin Meg?" asked the Queen, taking a curule chair as she spoke—the only one in the room.

"Nay, Lady. 'Tis mine hour for repeating the

seven penitential psalms. I have no time to waste with these giglots."

"Then, I pray you, give me leave to abide here myself for a season."

"You will do your pleasure, Lady. I only pray of you to keep them from laughing and such like wickedness."

"Nay, for I will not promise that for myself," said Queen Blanche, with a good-tempered smile. "Go your ways, Meg; we will work no evil."

The Countess turned and stalked out of the door again. And Clarice's first castle in the air fell into pieces behind her.

"Now, Agatha, I pray thee shut the door," said the Queen, "that we offend not my Cousin Margaret's ears in her psalms. Fare ye all well, my maids? Thy face is strange to me, child."

Clarice courtesied very low. "If it please the Lady Queen, I am but just come hither."

She had to tell her name and sundry biographical particulars, and then, suddenly looking round, the Queen said, "And where is Heliet?"

"Please it the Lady Queen, in my chamber," said Mistress Underdone.

"Bid her hither, good Agatha—if she can come."

"That can she, Lady."

Mistress Underdone left the room, and in another minute the regular tap of approaching crutches was audible. Clarice imagined their wearer to be some old woman—perhaps the mother of Mistress Underdone. But as soon as the door was opened again, she was surprised and touched to perceive that the sufferer who used them was a girl little older than herself. She came up to Queen Blanche, who welcomed her with a smile, and held her hand to the girl's lips to be kissed. This was her only way of paying homage, for to her courtesying and kneeling were alike impossible.

Clarice felt intuitively, as she looked into Heliet's face, that here was a girl entirely different from the rest. She seemed as if Nature had intended her to be tall, but had stopped and stunted her when only half grown. Her shoulders were unnaturally high, and one leg was considerably shorter than the other. Her face was not in any way beautiful, yet there was a certain mysterious attraction about it. Something looked out of her eyes which Clarice studied without being able to define, but which disposed her to keep on looking. They were dark, pathetic eyes, of the kind with which Clarice had gifted her very imaginary Countess; but there was something beyond the pathos.

"It looks," thought Clarice, "as if she had gone *through* the pathos and the suffering, and had come out on the other side—on the shore of the Golden Land, where they see what everything meant, and are satisfied."

There was very little time for conversation before the supper-bell rang. Queen Blanche made kind inquiries concerning Heliet's lameness and general

health, but had not reached any other subject when
the sound of the bell thrilled through the room.
The four girls rapidly folded up their work, as though
the summons were welcome. Queen Blanche rose
and departed, with a kindly nod to all, and Heliet,
turning to Clarice, said,

"Wilt thou come down with me? I cannot go
fast, as thou mayest see; but thou wilt sit next to
me, and I can tell thee anything thou mayest wish
to know."

Clarice thankfully assented, and they went down
the spiral staircase together into the great hall,
where three tables were spread. At the highest and
smallest, on the daïs, were already seated the Queen
and the Countess, two gentlemen, and two priests.
At the head of the second stood Mistress Underdone, next to whom was Diana, and Heliet led up
Clarice to her side. They faced the daïs, so that
Clarice could watch its distinguished occupants at
her pleasure. Tables for meals, at that date, were
simply boards placed on trestles, and removed when
the repast was over. On the table at the daïs was
silver plate, then a rare luxury, restricted to the
highest classes, the articles being spoons, knives,
plates, and goblets. There were no forks, for only
one fork had ever then been heard of as a thing
to eat with, and this had been the invention of the
wife of a Doge of Venice, about two hundred years
previous, for which piece of refinement the public
rewarded the lady by considering her as proud as

Lucifer. Forks existed, both in the form of spice-forks and fire-forks, but no one ever thought of eating with them in England until they were introduced from Italy in the reign of James I., and for some time after that the use of them marked either a traveller, or a luxurious, effeminate man. Moreover, there were no knives nor spoons provided for helping one's self from the dishes. Each person had a knife and spoon for himself, with which he helped himself at his convenience. People who were very delicate and particular wiped their knives on a piece of bread before doing so, and licked their spoons all over. When these were the practices of fastidious people, the proceedings of those who were not such may be discreetly left to imagination. The second table was served in a much more ordinary manner. In this instance the knife was iron and the spoon pewter, the plate a wooden trencher (never changed), and the drinking-cup of horn. In the midst of the table stood a pewter salt-cellar, formed like a castle, and very much larger than we use them now.

This salt-cellar acted as a barometer, not for weather, but for rank. Every one of noble blood, or filling certain offices, sat above the salt.

With respect to cooking our fathers had some peculiarities. They ate many things that we never touch, such as porpoises and herons, and they used all manner of green things as vegetables. They liked their bread hot from the oven (to give cold bread, even for dinner, was a shabby proceeding), and their meat much underdone, for they thought that overdone meat stirred up anger. They mixed most incongruous things together; they loved very strong tastes, delighting in garlic and verjuice; they never appear to have paid the slightest regard to their digestion, and they were, in the most emphatic sense, not teetotallers.

The dining-hall, but not the table, was decorated with flowers, and singers, often placed in a gallery at one end, were employed the whole time. A gentleman usher acted as butler, and a yeoman was always at hand to keep out strange dogs, snuff candles, and light to bed the guests, who were not always in a condition to find their way upstairs without his help. The hours at this time were nine or ten o'clock for dinner (except on fast-days, when it was at noon), and three or four for supper. Two meals a day were thought sufficient for all men who were not invalids. The sick and women sometimes had a "rear-supper" at six o'clock or later. As to breakfast, it was a meal taken only by some persons, and then served in the bedchamber or private boudoir at convenience. Wine, with bread sopped in it, was a favourite breakfast, especially for the old. Very delicate or exceptionally temperate people took milk for breakfast; but though the Middle Ages present us with examples of both vegetarians and total abstainers, yet of both there were very few indeed, and they were mainly to be found among the religious orders.

In watching the illustrious persons on the daïs one

thing struck Clarice as extremely odd, which would never be thought strange in the nineteenth century. It was the custom in her day for husband and wife to sit together at a meal, and, the highest ranks excepted, to eat from the same plate. But the Earl and Countess of Cornwall were on opposite sides of the table, with one of the priests between them. Clarice thought they must have quarrelled, and softly demanded of Heliet if that were the case.

"No, indeed," was Heliet's rather sorrowful answer. "At least, not more than usual. The Lady of Cornwall will never sit beside her baron, and, as thou shalt shortly see, she will not even speak to him."

"Not speak to him!" exclaimed Clarice.

"I never heard her do so yet," said Heliet.

"Does he entreat her very harshly?"

"There are few gentlemen more kindly or generous towards a wife. Nay, the harsh treatment is all on her side."

"What a miserable life to live!" commented Clarice.

"I fear he finds it so," said Heliet.

The dillegrout, or white soup, was now brought in, and Clarice, being hungry, attended more to her supper than to her mistress for a time. But during the next interval between the courses she studied her master.

He was a tall and rather fine-looking man, with a handsome face and a gentle, pleasant expression. There certainly was not in his exterior any cause for

repulsion. His hair was light, his eyes bluish-grey.
He seemed—or Clarice thought so at first—a silent
man, who left conversation very much to others; but
the decidedly intelligent glances of the grey eyes,
and an occasional twinkle of fun in them when any
amusing remark was made, showed that he was not
in the least devoid of brains.

Clarice thought that the priest who sat between
the Earl and Countess was a far more unpre-
possessing individual than his master. He was a
Franciscan friar, in the robe of his order; while the
friar who sat on the other side of the Countess was a
Dominican, and much more agreeable to look at.

At this juncture the Earl of Lancaster, who bore a
strong family likeness to his cousin, the Earl of Cornwall—a likeness which extended to character no less
than person—inquired of the latter if any news had
been heard lately from France.

"I have had no letters lately," replied his host;
and, turning to the Countess, he asked, "Have you,
Lady?"

Now, thought Clarice, she must speak to him.
Much to her surprise, the Countess, imagining, apparently, that the Franciscan friar was her ques-
tioner, answered,[1] "None, holy Father."

The friar gravely turned his head and repeated the
words to the Earl, though he must have heard them.

---

[1] This strange habit of the Countess is a fact, and sorely distressed the
Earl, as he has himself put on record, though with all his annoyance he
shows himself quite conscious of the comicality of the proceeding.

And Clarice became aware all at once that her own puzzled face was a source of excessive amusement to her *vis-à-vis*, Elaine. Her eyes inquired the reason.

"Oh, I know!" said Elaine, in a loud whisper across the table. "I know what perplexes thee. They are all like that when they first come. It is such fun to watch them!"

And she did not succeed in repressing a convulsion behind her handkerchief, even with the aid of Diana's "Elaine! do be sensible."

"Hush, my maid," said Mistress Underdone, gently. "If the Lady see thee laugh"——

"I shall be sent away without more supper, I know," said Elaine, shrugging her shoulders. "It is Clarice who ought to be punished, not I. I cannot help laughing when she looks so funny."

Elaine having succeeded in recovering her gravity without attracting the notice of the Countess, Clarice devoured her helping of salt beef along with much cogitation concerning her mistress's singular ways. Still, she could not restrain a supposition that the latter must have supposed the priest to speak to her, when she heard the Earl say, " I hear from Geoffrey Spenser [1] that our stock of salt ling is beyond what is like to be wanted. Methinks the villeins might have a cade or two thereof, my Lady."

And again, turning to the friar, the Countess made answer, "It shall be seen to, holy Father;" while the

[1] The *dépenseur*, or family provider. Hence comes the name of Le Despenser, which, therefore, should not be spelt Despencer.

friar, with equal composure, as though it were quite a matter of course, repeated to the Earl, " The Lady will see to it, my Lord."

" Does she always answer him so ? " demanded Clarice of Heliet, in an astonished whisper.

" Always," replied Heliet, with a sad smile.

" But surely," said Clarice, her amazement getting the better of her shyness, "it must be very wanting in reverence from a dame to her baron ! "

Clarice's ideas of wifely duty were of a very primitive kind. Unbounded reverence, unreasoning obedience, and diligent care for the husband's comfort and pleasure were the main items. As for love, in the sense in which it is usually understood now, that was an item which simply might come into the question, but it was not necessary by any means. Parents, at that time, kept it out of the matter as much as possible, and regarded it as more of an encumbrance than anything else.

" It is a very sad tale, Clarice," answered Heliet, in a low tone. " He loves her, and would cherish her dearly if she would let him. But there is not any love in her. When she was a young maid, almost a child, she set her heart on being a nun, and I think she has never forgiven her baron for being the innocent means of preventing her. I scarcely know which of them is the more to be pitied."

" Oh, he, surely ! " exclaimed Clarice.

" Nay, I am not so sure. God help those who are unloved ! but, far more, God help those who cannot love! I think she deserves the more compassion of the two."

"May be," answered Clarice, slowly—her thoughts were running so fast that her words came with hesitation. "But what shouldst thou say to one that had outlived a sorrowful love, and now thought it a happy chance that it had turned out contrary thereto?"

"It would depend upon how she had outlived it," responded Heliet, gravely.

"I heard one say, not many days gone," remarked Clarice—not meaning to let Heliet know from whom she had heard it—"that when she was young she loved a squire of her father, which did let her from wedding with him; and that now she was right thankful it so were, for he was killed on the field, and left never a plack behind him, and she was far better off, being now wed unto a gentleman of wealth and substance. What shouldst thou say to that?"

"If it were one of any kin to thee I would as lief say nothing to it," was Heliet's rather dry rejoinder.

"Nay, heed not that; I would fain know."

"Then I think the squire may have loved her, but so did she never him."

"In good sooth," said Clarice, "she told me she slept many a night on a wet pillow."

"So have I seen a child that had broken his toy," replied Heliet, smiling.

Clarice saw pretty plainly that Heliet thought such a state of things was not love at all.

"But how else can love be outlived?" she said.

" Love cannot.   But sorrow may be."

" Some folks say love and sorrow be nigh· the same."

" Nay, 'tis sin and sorrow that be nigh the same. All selfishness is sin, and very much of what men do commonly call love is but pure selfishness."

" Well, I never loved none yet," remarked Clarice

" God have mercy on thee ! " answered Heliet.

" Wherefore ? " demanded Clarice, in surprise.

" Because," said Heliet, softly, "' he that loveth not knoweth not God, for God is charity.' "

" Art thou destined for the cloister ? " asked Clarice.

Only priests, monks, and nuns, in her eyes, had any business to talk religiously, or might reasonably be expected to do so.

" I am destined to fulfil that which is God's will for me," was Heliet's simple reply.   " Whether that will be the cloister or no I have not yet learned."

Clarice cogitated upon this reply while she ate stewed apples.

" Thou hast an odd name," she said, after a pause.

" What, Heliet ? " asked its bearer, with a smile. " It is taken from the name of the holy prophet Elye,[1] of old time."

" Is it ?   But I mean the other."

" Ah, I love it not," said Heliet.

" No, it is very queer," replied Clarice, with an apologetic blush, " very odd—Underdone ! "

[1] Elijah.

"Oh, but that is not my name," answered Heliet, quickly, with a little laugh; "but it is quite as bad. It is Pride."

Clarice fancied she had heard the name before, but she could not remember where.

"But why is it bad?" said she. "Then I reckon Mistress Underdone hath been twice wed?"

"She hath," said Heliet, answering the last question first, as people often do, "and my father was her first husband. Why is pride evil? Surely thou knowest that."

"Oh, I know it is one of the seven deadly sins, of course," responded Clarice, quickly; "still it is very necessary and noble."

Heliet's smile expressed a mixture of feelings. Clarice was not the first person who has held one axiom theoretically, but has practically behaved according to another.

"The Lord saith that He hates pride," said the lame girl, softly. "How, then, can it be necessary, not to say noble?"

"Oh, but ——" Clarice went no further.

"But He did not mean what He said?"

"Oh, yes, of course!" said Clarice. "But"——

"Better drop the *but*," said Heliet, quaintly. "And Father Bevis is about to say grace."

The Dominican friar rose and returned thanks for the repast, and the company broke up, the Earl and Countess, with their guests, leaving the hall by the upper door, while the household retired by the lower.

The preparations for sleep were almost as primitive as those for meals. Exalted persons, such as the Earl and Countess, slept in handsome bedsteads, of the tent form, hung with silk curtains, and spread with coverlets of fur, silk, or tapestry. They washed in silver basins, with ewers of the same costly metal; and they sat, the highest rank in curule chairs, the lower upon velvet-covered forms or stools. But ordinary people, of whom Clarice was one, were not provided for in this luxurious style. Bower-maidens slept in pallet-beds, which were made extremely low, so as to run easily under one of the larger bedsteads, and thus be put out of the way. All beds rejoiced in a quantity of pillows. Our ancestors made much more use of pillows and cushions than we—a fact easily accounted for, considering that they had no softly-stuffed chairs, but only upright ones of hard carved wood. But Clarice's sheets were simple "cloth of Rennes," while those of her mistress were set with jewels. Her mattress was stuffed with hay instead of wool; she had neither curtains nor fly-nets, and her coverlet was of plain cloth, unwrought by the needle. In the matter of blankets they fared alike except as to quality. But in the bower-maidens' chamber, where all the girls slept together, there were no basins of any material. Early in the morning a strong-armed maid came in, bearing a tub of water, which she set down on one of the coffers of carved oak which stood at the foot of each bed and held all the personal treasures of

THE MISTS CLEAR AWAY.

the sleeper. Then, by means of a mop which she
brought with her, she gently sprinkled every face
with water, thus intimating that it was time to get
up. The tub she left behind. It was to provide—
on the principle of "first come, first served"—for
the ablutions of all the five young ladies, though
each had her personal towel. Virtue was thus its
own reward, the laziest girl being obliged to content
herself with the dirtiest water. It must, however, be
remembered that she was a fastidious damsel who
washed more than face and hands.

They then dressed themselves, carefully tying
their respective amulets round their necks, without
which proceeding they would have anticipated all
manner of ill luck to befall them during the day.
These articles were small boxes of the nature of a
locket, containing either a little dust of one saint, a
shred of the conventual habit of another, or a few
verses from a gospel, written very minutely, and
folded up extremely small. Then each girl, as she
was ready, knelt in the window, and gabbled over in
Latin, which she did not understand, a Paternoster,
ten Aves, and the Angelical Salutation, not unfrequently breaking eagerly into the conversation
almost before the last Amen had left her lips.
Prayers over, they passed into the sitting-room
next door, where they generally found a basket of
manchet bread and biscuits, with a large jug of ale
or wine. A gentleman usher called for Mistress
Underdone and her charges, and conducted them

to mass in the chapel. Here they usually found
the Earl and Countess before them, who alone,
except the priests, were accommodated with seats.
Each girl courtesied first to the altar, then to the
Countess, and lastly to the Earl, before she took
her allotted place. The Earl always returned the
salutation by a quiet inclination of his head. The
Countess sat in stony dignity, and never took any
notice of it. Needlework followed until dinner, after
which the Countess gave audience for an hour to
any person desiring to see her, and usually concluded it by a half-hour's nap. Further needlework,
for such as were not summoned to active attendance
on their mistress if she went out, lasted until vespers,
after which supper was served. After supper was
the recreation time, when in most houses the bower-
maidens enjoyed themselves with the gentlemen of
the household in games or dancing in the hall;
but the Lady Margaret strictly forbade any such
frivolous doings in her maidens. They were still
confined to their own sitting-room, except on some
extraordinary occasion, and the only amusements
allowed them were low-toned conversation, chess,
draughts, or illumination. Music, dancing (even by
the girls alone), noisy games of all kinds, and laughter,
the Countess strictly tapued. The practical result
was that the young ladies fell back upon gossip and
ghost-stories, until there were few nights in the year
when Roisia would have dared to go to bed by herself for a king's ransom. An hour before bed-time

wine and cakes were served. After this Mistress Underdone recited the Rosary, the girls making the responses, and at eight o'clock—a late hour at that time—they trooped off to bed. All were expected to be in bed and all lights out by half-past eight. The unlucky maiden who loitered or was accidentally hindered had to finish her undressing in the dark.

CHAPTER III.

ON THE THRESHOLD OF LIFE.

"I will not dream of him handsome and strong,—
　My ideal love may be weak and slight;
It matters not to what class he belong,
　He would be noble enough in my sight;
But he must be courteous toward the lowly,
　To the weak and sorrowful, loving too;
He must be courageous, refined, and holy,
　By nature exalted, and firm, and true."

Y the time that Clarice had been six weeks at Oakham she had pretty well made up her mind as to the characters of her companions. The Countess did not belie the estimate formed on first seeing her. The gentle, mournful, loving woman of Clarice's dreams had vanished, never to be recalled. The girl came to count that a red-letter day on which she did not see her mistress. Towards the Earl her feeling was an odd mixture of reverential liking and compassion. He came far nearer the ideal picture than his wife. His manners were unusually gentle and considerate of others, and he was specially remarkable for one trait very rarely found in the Middle Ages—he was always

thoughtful of those beneath him. Another peculiarity he had, not common in his time; he was decidedly a humourist. The comic side even of his own troubles was always patent to him. Yet he was a man of extremely sensitive feeling, as well as of shrewd and delicate perceptions. He lived a most uncomfortable life, and he was quite aware of it. The one person who should have been his truest friend deliberately nursed baseless enmity towards him. The only one whom he loved in all the world hated him with deadly hatred. And there was no cause for it but one—the strongest cause of all—the reason why Cain slew his brother. He was of God, and she was of the world. Yet nothing could have persuaded her that he was not on the high road to perdition, while she was a special favourite of Heaven.

Clarice found Mistress Underdone much what she had expected—a good-natured, sensible supervisor. Her position, too, was not an easy one. She had to submit her sense to the orders of folly, and to sink her good-nature in submission to harshness. But she did her best, steered as delicately as she could between her Scylla and Charybdis, and always gave her girls the benefit of a doubt.

The girls themselves were equally distinct as to character. Olympias was delicate, with a failing of delicate people—a disposition to complaining and fault-finding. Elaine was full of fun, ready to barter any advantage in the future for enjoyment in the

present. Diana was caustic, proud of her high con-
nections, which were a shade above those of her
companions, and inclined to be scornful towards
everything not immediately patent to her comprehension. Roisia, while the most amiable, was also
the weakest in character of the four; she was easily
led astray by Elaine, easily persuaded to deviate
from the right through fear of Diana.

The two priests had also unfolded themselves.
The Dominican, Father Bevis, awoke in Clarice a
certain amount of liking, not unmixed with rather
timorous respect. But he was a grave, silent, un-
demonstrative man, who gave no encouragement to
anything like personal affection, though he was not
harsh nor unkind. The Franciscan, Father Miles,
was of a type common in his day. The man and
the priest were two different characters. Father
Miles in the confessional was a stern master; Father
Miles at the supper-table was a jovial playfellow.
In his eyes, religion was not the breath and salt of
life, but something altogether separate from it, and
only to be mentioned on a Sunday. It was a bundle
of ceremonies, not a living principle. To Father
Bevis, on the contrary, religion was everything or
nothing. If it had anything to do with a man at all,
it must pervade his thoughts and his life. It was the
leaven which leavened the whole lump; the salt
whose absence left all unsavoury and insipid; the
breath, which virtually was identical with life. One
mistake Father Bevis made, a very natural mistake

to a man who had been repressed, misunderstood, and disliked, as he had been ever since he could remember—he did not realise sufficiently that warmth was a necessity of life, and that young creatures more especially required a certain brooding tenderness to develope their faculties. No one had ever given him love but God; and he was too apt to suppose that religion could be fostered only in that way which had cherished his own. His light burned bright to Godward, but it was not sufficiently visible to men.

Clarice La Theyn had by this time discovered that there were other people in the household beyond those already mentioned. The Earl had four squires of the body, and the Countess two pages in waiting, beside a meaner crowd of dressers, sewers, porters, messengers, and all kinds of officials. The squires and the pages were the only ones who came much in contact with the bower-maidens.

Both the pages were boys of about fifteen, of whom Osbert was quiet and sedate for a boy, while Jordan was *espiègle* and full of mischievous tricks. The squires demand longer notice.

Reginald de Echingham was the first to attract Clarice's notice—a fact which, in Reginald's eyes, would only have been natural and proper. He was a handsome young man, and no one was better aware of it than himself. His principal virtue lay in a silky moustache, which he perpetually caressed. The Earl called him Narcissus, and he deserved it.

Next came Fulk de Chaucombe, who was about as careless of his personal appearance as Reginald was careful. He looked on his brother squire with ineffable disdain, as a man only fit to hunt out rhymes for sonnets, and hold skeins of silk for ladies. Call him a man! thought Master Fulk, with supreme contempt. Fulk's notion of manly occupations centred in war, with an occasional tournament by way of dessert.

Third on the list was Vivian Barkworth. To Clarice, at least, he was a perplexity. He was so chameleon-like that she could not make up her mind about him. He could be extremely attractive when he liked, and he could be just as repellent.

Least frequently of any were her thoughts given to Ademar de Gernet. She considered him at first entirely colourless. He was not talkative; he was neither handsome nor ugly; he showed no special characteristic which would serve to label him. She merely put him on one side, and never thought of him unless she happened to see him.

Her fellow bower-maidens also had their ideas concerning these young gentlemen. Olympias was—or fancied herself—madly in love with the handsome Reginald, on whom Elaine cracked jokes and played tricks, and Diana exhausted all her satire. As to Reginald, he was too deeply in love with himself to be sensible of the attractions of any other person. It struck Clarice as very odd when she found that the weak and gentle Roisia was a timid admirer of the bear-like De Chaucombe. As for Diana, her shafts were levelled impartially at all; but in her inmost heart Clarice fancied that she liked Vivian Barkeworth. Elaine was heart-whole, and plainly showed it.

The Countess had not improved on further acquaintance. She was not only a tyrant, but a capricious one. Not merely was penalty sure to follow on not pleasing her, but it was not easy to say what would please her at any given moment.

" We might as well be in a nunnery !" exclaimed Diana.

" Nay," said Elaine, " for then we could not get out."

" Don't flatter thyself on getting out, pray," returned Diana. " We shall never get out except by marrying, or really going into a nunnery."

" For which I am sure I have no vocation," laughed Elaine. " Oh, no ! I shall marry; and won't I lead my baron a dance !"

" Who is it to be, Elaine ?" asked Clarice.

" *Ha, chétife !* How do I know? The Lady will settle that. I only hope it won't be a man who puts oil on his hair and scents himself."

This remark was a side-thrust at Reginald, as Olympias well knew, and she looked reproachfully at Elaine.

" Well, I hope it won't be one who kills half-a-dozen men every morning before breakfast," said Diana, making a hit at Fulk.

D

It was Roisia's turn to look reproachful. Clarice could not help laughing.

"What dost thou think of our giddy speeches, Heliet?" said she.

Heliet looked up with her bright smile.

"Very like maidens' fancies," she said. "For me, I am never like to wed, so I can look on from the outside."

"But what manner of man shouldst thou fancy, Heliet?"

"Oh aye, do tell us!" cried more than one voice.

"I warrant he'll be a priest," said Elaine.

"He will have fair hair and soft manners," remarked Olympias.

"Nay, he shall have such hair as shall please God," said Heliet, more gravely. "But he must be gentle and loving, above all to the weak and sorrowful: a true knight, to whom every woman is a holy thing, to be guarded and tended with care. He must put full affiance in God, and love Him supremely: and next, me; and below that, all other. He must not fear danger, yet without fool-hardiness; but he must fear disgrace, and fear and hate sin. He must be true to himself, and must aim at making of himself the best man that ever he can. He must not be afraid of ridicule, or of being thought odd. He must have firm convictions, and be ready to draw sword for them, without looking to see whether other men be on the same side or not. His heart must be open to all misery, his brain to all true and innocent knowledge, his hand ready to redress every wrong not done to himself. For his enemies he must have forgiveness ; for his friends, unswerving constancy : for all men, courtesy."

"And that is thy model man ? *Ha, jolife!*" cried Elaine. "Why, I could not stand a month of him."

"I am afraid he would be rather soft and flat," said Diana, with a curl of her lip.

"No, I don't think that," answered Roisia. "But I should like to know where Heliet expects to find him."

"Do give his address, Heliet!" said Elaine, laughing.

"Ah! I never knew but one that answered to that description," was Heliet's reply.

"*Ha, jolife!*" cried Elaine, clapping her hands. "Now for his name! I hope I know him—but I am sure I don't."

"You all know His name," said Heliet, gravely "How many of us know *Him?* For indeed, I know of no such man that ever lived, except only Jesus Christ our Lord."

There was no answer. A hush seemed to have fallen on the whole party, which was at last broken by Olympias.

"Well, but—thou knowest we cannot have Him."

"Pardon me, I know no such thing," answered Heliet, in the same soft, grave tone. "Does not the Psalmist say, '*Portio mea, Domine*'?[1] And does

[1] "Thou art my portion, O Lord."—Ps. cxix. 57.

not Solomon say, '*Dilectus meus mihi'?*[1]   Is it not
the very glory of His infinitude, that all who are His
can have all of Him?"

"Where did Heliet pick up these queer notions?"
said Diana under her breath.

"She goes to such extremes!" Elaine whispered
back.

"But all that means to go into the cloister," replied
Olympias in a discontented tone.

"Nay," said Heliet, taking up her crutches, "I
hope a few will go to Heaven who do not go into the
cloister.   But we may rest assured of this, that not
one will go there who has not chosen Christ for his
portion."

"Well," said Diana, calmly, a minute after Heliet
had disappeared, "I suppose she means to be a nun!
But she might let that alone till she is one."

"Let what alone?" asked Roisia.

"Oh, all that parson's talk," returned Diana.   "It
is all very well for priests and nuns, but secular
people have nothing to do with it."

"I thought even secular people wanted to go to
Heaven," coolly put in Elaine, not because she cared
a straw for the question, but because she delighted in
taking the opposite side to Diana.

"Let them go, then!" responded Diana, rather
sharply.   "They can keep it to themselves, can't
they?"

"Well, I don't know," said Elaine, laughing.

---

[1] "My beloved is mine."—Cant. ii. 16.

"Some people cannot keep things to themselves. Just look at Olympias, whatever she is doing, how she argues the whole thing out in public. 'Oh, shall I go or not? Yes, I think I will; no, I won't, though; yes, but I will; oh, can't somebody tell me what to do?'"

Elaine's mimicry was so perfect that Olympias herself joined in the laugh. The last-named damsel carried on all her mental processes in public, instead of presenting her neighbours, as most do, with results only. And when people wear their hearts upon their sleeves, the daws will come and peck at them.

"Now, don't tease Olympias," said Roisia good-naturedly.

"Oh, let one have a bit of fun," said Elaine, "when one lives in a convent of the strictest order."

"I suspect thou wouldst find a difference if thou wert to enter one," sneered Diana.

Elaine would most likely have fought out the question had not Mistress Underdone entered at that moment with a plate of gingerbread in her hand smoking hot from the oven.

"Oh, Mistress, I am so hungry!" plaintively observed that young lady.

Mistress Underdone laughed, and set down the plate. "There, part the spice-cake among you," said she. "And when you be through, I have somewhat to tell you."

"Tell us now," said Elaine, as well as a mouthful of gingerbread allowed her to speak.

"Let me see, now—what day is this?" inquired Mistress Underdone.

All the voices answered her at once, "St. Dunstan's Eve!"[1]

"So it is. Well—come St. Botulph,[2] as I have but now learned, we go to Whitehall."

"*Ha, jolife!*" cried Diana, Elaine, and Roisia at once.

"Will Heliet go too?" asked Clarice, softly.

"Oh, no; Heliet never leaves Oakham," responded Olympias.

Mistress Underdone looked kindly at Clarice. "No, Heliet will not go," she said. "She cannot ride, poor heart." And the mother sighed, as if she felt the prospective pain of separation.

"But there will be dozens of other maidens," said Elaine. "There are plenty of girls in the world beside Heliet."

Clarice was beginning to think there hardly were for her.

"Oh, thou dost not know what thou wilt see at Westminster!" exclaimed Elaine. "The Lord King, and the Lady Queen, and all the Court; and the Abbey, with all its riches, and ever so many maids and gallants. It is delicious beyond description, when the Lady is away visiting some shrine, and she does that nearly every day."

Roisia's "Hush!" had come too late.

"I pray you say that again, my mistress!" said

[1] May 13.   [2] June 17.

the well-known voice of the Lady Margaret in the doorway. " Nay, I will have it.—Fetch me the rod, Agatha.—Now then, minion, what saidst? Thou caitiff giglot! If I had thee not in hand, that tongue of thine should bring thee to ruin. What saidst, hussy ? "

And Elaine had to repeat the unlucky words, with the birch in prospect, and immediately afterwards in actuality.

" I will lock thee up when I go visiting shrines ! " said the Countess with her last stroke. " Agatha, remember when we are at Westminster that I have said so."

" Aye, Lady," observed Mistress Underdone, com· posedly.

And the Lady Margaret, throwing down the birch, stalked away, and left the sobbing Elaine to resume her composure at her leisure.

In a vaulted upper chamber of the Palace of Westminster, on a bright morning in June, four persons were seated. Three, who were of the nobler sex, were engaged in converse; the last, a lady, sat apart with her embroidery in modest silence. They were near relatives, for the men were respectively husband, brother-in-law, and uncle of the woman, and they were the most prominent members of the royal line of England, with one who did not belong to it.

Foremost of the group was the King. He was

foremost in more senses than one, for, as is well
known, Edward I., like Saul, was higher than any of
his people.   Moreover, he was as spare as he was
tall, which made him look almost gigantic.   His
forehead was large and broad, his features handsome and regular, but marred by that perpetual
droop in his left eyelid which he had inherited from
his father.   Hair and complexion, originally fair, had
been bronzed by his Eastern campaigns till the crisp
curling hair was almost black, and the delicate tint
had acquired a swarthy hue.   He had a nose inclin-
ing to the Roman type, a broad chest, agile arms,
and excessively long legs.   His dark eyes were soft
when he was in a good temper, but fierce as a tiger's
when roused to anger; and His Majesty's temper
was—well, not precisely angelic.[1]   It was like lightning, in being as sudden and fierce, but it did not
resemble that natural phenomenon in disappearing
as quickly as it had come.   On the contrary, Edward
never forgot and hardly forgave an injury.   His

---

[1] Two anecdotes may be given which illustrate this in a manner
almost comical; the first has been published more than once, the latter
has not to my knowledge.   When his youngest daughter Elizabeth was
married to the Earl of Hereford in 1302, the King, annoyed by some
unfortunate remark of the bride, snatched her coronet from her head
and threw it into the fire, nor did the Princess recover it undamaged.
In 1305, writing to John de Fonteyne, the physician of his second wife,
Marguerite of France, who was then ill of small-pox, the King warns
him not on any account to allow the Queen to exert herself until she has
completely recovered, "and if you do," adds the monarch in French,
of considerably more force than elegance, and not too suitable for exact
quotation, "you shall pay for it !"

abilities were beyond question, and, for his time, he was an unusually independent and original thinker. His moral character, however, was worse than is commonly supposed, though it did not descend to the lowest depths it reached until after the death of his fair and faithful Leonor.

The King's brother Edmund was that same Earl of Lancaster whom we have already seen at Oakham. He was a man of smaller intellectual calibre than his royal brother, but of much pleasanter disposition. Extreme gentleness was his principal characteristic, as it has been that of all our royal Edmunds, though in some instances it degenerated into excessive weakness. This was not the case with the Earl of Lancaster. His great kindness of heart is abundantly attested by his own letters and his brother's State papers.

William de Valence, Earl of Pembroke, was the third member of the group, and he was the uncle of the royal brothers, being a son of their grandmother's second marriage with Hugh de Lusignan, Count de La Marche. Though he made a deep mark upon his time, yet his character is not easy to fathom beyond two points—that his ability had in it a little element of craft, and that he took reasonable care of Number One.

Over the head of the lady who sat in the curule chair, quietly embroidering, twenty-five years had passed since she had been styled by a poet, "the loveliest lady in all the land." She was hardly less

even now, when her fifty years were nearly numbered ; when, unseen by any earthly eyes, her days
were drawing to their close, and the angel of death
stood close beside her, ready to strike before six
months should be fulfilled. Certainly, according to
modern ideas of beauty, never was a queen fairer
than Leonor the Faithful, and very rarely has there
been one as fair. And—more unusual still—she was
as good as she was beautiful. The worst loss in all
her husband's life was the loss of her.

So far from seeing any sorrow looming in the
future was King Edward at this moment, that he
was extremely jubilant over a project which he
had just brought to a successful issue.

"There !" said he, rubbing his hands in supreme
satisfaction, "that parchment settles the business
When both my brother of Scotland and I are gone,
our children will reign over one empire, king and
queen of both. Is not that worth living for ? "

" *Soit !* " [1] ejaculated De Valence, shrugging his
Provençal shoulders. "A few acres of bare moss and
a handful of stags, to say nothing of the barbarians
who dwell up in those misty regions. A fine matter
surely to clap one's hands over ! "

"Ah, fair uncle, you never travelled in Scotland,"
interposed the gentle Lancaster, before the King
could blaze up, "and you know not what sort of
country it is. From what I have heard, it would
easily match your land in respect of beauty."

[1] Be it so.

"Match Poitou? or Provence? Cousin, you must have taken leave of your senses. You were not born on the banks of the Isère, or you would not chatter such treason as that."

"Truly no, fair Uncle, for I was born in the City of London, just beyond," said Lancaster, with a good-humoured laugh; "and, verily, that would rival neither Scotland nor Poitou, to say nothing of Dauphiné and Provence. The goddess of beauty was not in attendance when I was born."

Perhaps few would have ventured on that assertion except himself. Edmund of Lancaster was among the most handsome of our princes.

"Beshrew you both!" cried King Edward, unfraternally; "wherever will these fellows ramble with their tongues? Who said anything about beauty? I care not, I, if the maiden Margaret were the ugliest lass that ever tied a kerchief, so long as she is the heiress of Scotland. Ned has beauty enough and to spare; let him stare in the glass if he cannot look at his wife."

The Queen looked up with an amused expression, and would, perhaps, have spoken, had not the tapestry been lifted by some person unseen, and a little boy of six years old bounded into the room.

No wonder that the fire in the King's eyes died into instant softness. It would have been a wonder if the parents had not been proud of that boy, for he was one of the loveliest children on whom human eye ever rested. Did it ever cross the minds of that father and mother that the kindest deed they could have done to that darling child would have been to smother him in his cradle? Had the roll of his life been held up before them at that moment, they would have counted only thirty-seven years, written within and without in lamentation, and mourning, and woe.

King Edward lifted his little heir upon his knee.

"Look here, Ned," said he. "Seest yonder parchment?"

The blue eyes opened a little, and the fair curls shook with a nod of affirmation.

"What is it, thinkest?"

A shake of the pretty little head was the reply.

"Thy Cousin Margaret is coming to dwell with thee. That parchment will bring her."

"How old is she?" asked the Prince.

"But just a year younger than thou."

"Is she nice?"

The King laughed. "How can I tell thee? I never saw her."

"Will she play with us?"

"I should think she will. She is just between thee and Beatrice."

"Beatrice is only a baby!" remarked the Prince disdainfully. Six years old is naturally scornful of four.

"Not more of a baby than thou," said his uncle Lancaster, playfully.

"But she's a girl, and I'm a man!" cried the insulted little Prince.

King Edward, excessively amused, set his boy

down on the floor. "There, run to thy mother," said he. "Thou wilt be a man one of these days, I dare say; but not just yet, Master Ned."

And no angel voice whispered to one of them that it would have been well for that child if he had never been a man, nor that ere he was six months older, the mother, whose death was a worse calamity to him than to any other, and the little Norwegian lassie to whom he was now betrothed, would pass almost hand in hand into the silent land. Three months later, Margaret, Princess of Norway and Queen of Scotland, set sail from her father's coast for her mother's kingdom, whence she was to travel to England, and be brought up under the tender care of the royal Leonor as its future queen. But one of the sudden and terrible storms of the North Sea met her ere she reached the shore of Scotland. She just lived to be flung ashore at Kirkwall, in the Orkneys, and there, in the pitying hands of the fishers' wives, the child breathed out her little life, having lived five years, and reigned for nearly as long. Who of us, looking back to the probable lot that would have awaited her in England, shall dare to pity that little child?

CHAPTER IV.

WAITING AND WEARY.

"Oh! for the strength of God's right hand! the way is hard and
dreary,—
Through Him to walk and not to faint, to run and not be weary!"
—E. L. MARZIALS.

E left the Royal party in conversation in the
chamber at Westminster.

"Have you quite resolved, Sire, to expel
all the Jews from England?" asked De Valence.

"Resolved? Yes; I hope it is half done," replied the King. "You are aware, fair Uncle, that
our Commons voted us a fifteenth on this condition?"

"No, I did not hear that," said De Valence.

"How many are there of those creatures?" inquired Lancaster.

"How should I know?" returned Edward, with
an oath. "I only know that the Chancellor said the
houses and goods were selling well to our profit."

"Fifteen thousand and sixty, my Lord of Surrey
told me," said Lancaster. "I doubted if it were not
too high a computation; that is why I asked."

"Oh, very likely not," responded Edward, carelessly. "There are as many of them as gnats, and as much annoyance."

"Well, it is a pious deed, of course," said Lancaster, stroking his moustache, not in the dilettante style of De Echingham, but like a man lost in thought. "It seems a pity, though, for the women and children."

"My cousin of Lancaster, I do believe, sings *Dirige* over the chickens in his barnyard," sneered De Valence.

Lancaster looked up with a good-tempered smile.

"Does my fair Uncle never wish for the day when the lion shall eat straw like the ox?"[1]

"Not I!" cried De Valence, with a hearty laugh. "Why, what mean you? are we to dine on a haunch of lion when it comes?"

"Nay, for that were to make us worse than either, methinks. I suppose we shall give over eating what has had life, at that time."

"*Merci, mille fois!*" laughed his uncle. "My dinner will be spoiled. Not thine, I dare say. I'll be bound, Sire, our fair cousin will munch his apples and pears with all the gusto in the world, and send his squire to the stable to inquire if the lion has a straw doubled under him."

"Bah!" said the King. "What are you talking about?"

---

[1] Some readers will think such ideas too modern to have occurred to any one in 1290. There is evidence to the contrary.

" How much will this business of the Jews cost your Grace ?" asked De Valence, dropping his sarcasms.

" Cost *me ?*" demanded Edward, with a short laugh. " Did our fair uncle imagine we meant to execute such a project at our own expense ? Let the rogues pay their own travelling fees."

" Ha! good!" said the Poitevin noble. " And our fair cousin of Lancaster shall chant the *De Profundis* while they embark, and I will offer a silver fibula to St. Edward that they may all be drowned. How sayest, fair Cousin ?"

" Nay," was Lancaster's answer, in a doubtful tone. " I reckon we ought not to pity them, being they that crucified our Lord. But——"

But for all that, his heart cried out against his creed. Yet it did not occur to him that the particular men who were being driven from their homes for no fault of theirs, and forced with keen irony of oppression to pay their own expenses, were not those who crucified Christ, but were removed from them by many generations. The times of the Gentiles were not yet fulfilled, and the cry, " His blood be on us, *and on our children,*" had not yet exhausted its awful power.

There was one person not present who would heartily have agreed with Lancaster. This was his cousin and namesake, Edmund, Earl of Cornwall, who not only felt for the lower animals—a rare yet occasional state of mind in the thirteenth century—but went further, and compassionated the villeins—

a sentiment which very few indeed would have dreamed of sharing with him. The labourers on the land were serfs, and had no feelings,—that is, none that could be recognised by the upper classes. They were liable to be sold with the land which they tilled; nor could they leave their "hundred" without a passport. Their sons might not be educated to anything but agriculture; their daughters could not be married without paying a fine to the master. Worse things than these are told of some, for of course the condition of the serf largely depended on the disposition of his owner.

The journey from Oakham to Westminster was a pleasant change to all the bower-maidens but one, and that was the one selected to travel with her mistress in the litter. Each was secretly, if not openly, hoping not to be that one; and it was with no little trepidation that Clarice received the news that this honour was to be conferred on her. She discovered, however, on the journey, that scolding was not the perpetual occupation of the Countess. She spent part of every day in telling her beads, part in reading books wofully dry to the apprehension of Clarice, and part in sleeping, which not unfrequently succeeded the beads. Conversation she never attempted, and Clarice, who dared not speak till she was spoken to, began to entertain a fear of losing the use of her tongue. Otherwise she was grave and quiet enough, poor girl! for she was not naturally talkative. She was very sorry to part with Heliet, and she felt, almost without knowing why, some apprehension concerning the future. Sentiments of this sort were quite unknown to such girls as Elaine, Diana, and Roisia, while with Olympias they arose solely from delicate health. But Clarice was made of finer porcelain, and she could not help mournfully feeling that she had not a friend in the world. Her father and mother were not friends; they were strangers who might be expected to do what they thought best for her, just as the authorities of a workhouse might take conscientious care in the apprenticing of the workhouse girls. But no more could be expected, and Clarice felt it. If there had only been, anywhere in the world, somebody who loved her! There was no such probability to which it was safe to look forward. Possibly, some twenty or thirty years hence, some of her children might love her. As for her husband, he was simply an embarrassing future certainty, who — with almost equal certainty—would not care a straw about her. That was only to be expected. The squire who liked Roisia would be pretty sure to get Diana; while the girl who admired Reginald de Echingham was safe to fall to Fulk de Chaucombe. Things always were arranged so in this world. Perhaps, thought Clarice, those girls were the happiest who did not care, who took life as it came, and made all the fun they could out of it. But she knew well that this was how life and she would never take each other.

Whitehall was reached at last, on the eve of St. Botolph. Clarice was excessively tired, and only able to judge of the noise without, and the superb decorations and lofty rooms within. Lofty, be it remembered, to her eyes; they would not look so to ours. She supped upon salt merling,[1] peasecods,[2] and stewed fruit, and was not sorry to get to bed.

In the morning, she found the household considerably increased. Her eyes were almost dazzled by the comers and goers; and she really noticed only one person. Two young knights were among the new attendants of the Earl, but one of them Clarice could not have distinguished from the crowd. The other had attracted her notice by coming forward to help the Countess from her litter, and, instead of attending his mistress further, had, rather to Clarice's surprise, turned to help *her*. And when she looked up to thank him, it struck her that his face was like somebody she knew. She did not discover who it was till Roisia observed, while the girls were undressing, that—"My cousin is growing a beard, I declare. He had none the last time I saw him."

" Which is thy cousin ?" asked Clarice.

"Why, Piers Ingham," said Roisia. " He that helped my Lady from the litter."

" Oh, is he thy cousin ?" responded Clarice.

" By the mother's side," answered Roisia. " He hath but been knighted this last winter."

" Then he is just ready for a wife," said Elaine.

---

[1] Whiting.   [2] Green peas.

" I wonder which of us it will be! It is tolerably sure to be one. I say, maids, I mean to have a jolly time of it while we are here! It shall go hard with me if I do not get promoted to be one of the Queen's bower-women!"

" Oh, would I?" interpolated Diana.

" Why?" asked more than one voice.

" I am sure," said Olympias, " I had ever so much rather be under the Lady Queen than our Lady."

"Oh, that may be," said Diana. " I was not looking at it in that light. There is some amusement in deceiving our Lady, and one doesn't feel it wrong, because she is such a vixen; but there would be no fun in taking in the Queen, she's too good."

" I wonder what Father Bevis would say to that doctrine," demurely remarked Elaine. " What it seems to mean is, that a lie is not such a bad thing if you tell it to a bad person as it would be if you told it to a good one. Now I doubt if Father Bevis would be quite of that opinion."

" Don't talk nonsense," was Diana's reply.

" Well, but is it nonsense? Didst thou mean that?"

It was rather unusual for Elaine thus to satirise Diana, and looked as if the two had changed characters, especially when Diana walked away, muttering something which no one distinctly heard.

Elaine proved herself a tolerably true prophetess. *Fête* followed *fête*. Clarice found herself initiated into Court circles, and discovered that she was enjoying herself very much. But whether the attraction lay in the pageants, in the dancing, in her own bright array, or in the companionship, she did not pause to ask herself. Perhaps if she had paused, and made the inquiry, she might have discovered that life had changed to her since she came to Westminster. The things eternal, of which Heliet alone had spoken to her, had faded away into far distance; they had been left behind at Oakham. The things temporal were becoming everything.

In a stone balcony overhanging the Thames, at Whitehall, sat Earl Edmund of Cornwall, in a thoughtful attitude, resting his head upon his hand. He had been alone for half an hour, but now a tall man, in a Dominican habit, who was not Father Bevis, came round the corner of the balcony, which ran all along that side of the house. He was the Prior or Rector of Ashbridge, a collegiate community, founded by the Earl himself, of which we shall hear more anon.

The Friar sat down on the stone bench near the Earl, who took no further notice of him than by a look, his eyes returning to dreamy contemplation of the river.

"Of what is my Lord thinking?" asked the Friar, gently.

"Of life," said the Prince.

"Not very hopefully, I imagine."

"The hope comes at the beginning, Father. Look

at yonder pleasure-boat, with the lads and lasses in
it, setting forth for a row.   There is hope enough in
their faces.   But when the journey comes near its
end, and the perilous bridge must be shot, and the
night is setting in, what you see in the faces then
will not be hope.   It will be weariness; perhaps disgust and sorrow.   And—in some voyages, the hope
dies early."

"True—if it has reference only to the day."

"Ah," responded the Prince, with a smile which
had more sadness than mirth in it, "you mean to
point me to the hope beyond.   But the day is long
Father.   The night has not come yet, and the bridge
is still to be shot.   Aye, and the wind and rain are
cold, as one drops slowly down the river."

"There is home at the end, nevertheless," answered
the Dominican.   "When we sit round the fire in
the banquet hall, and all we love are round us, and
the doors shut safe, we shall easily forget the cold
wind on the water."

"When!   Yes.   But I am on the water yet, and it
may be some hours before my barge is moored at the
garden steps.   And—it is always the same, Father.
It does seem strange, when there is only one earthly
thing for which a man cares, that God should deny
him that one thing.   Why rouse the hope which is
never to be fulfilled?   If the width of the world had
lain all our lives between me and my Lady, we
should both have been happier.   Why should God
bring us together to spoil each other's lives?   For I

dare say she is as little pleased with her lot as I with mine—poor Magot!"

"Will my Lord allow me to alter the figure he has chosen?" said the Predicant Friar. "Look at your own barge moored down below. If the rope were to break, what would become of the barge?"

"It would drift down the river."

"And if there were in it a little child, alone, too young to have either skill or strength to steer it, what would become of him when the barge shot the bridge?"

"Poor soul!—destruction, without question."

"And what if my Lord be that little child, safe as yet in the barge which the Master has tied fast to the shore? The rope is his trouble. What if it be his safety also? He would like far better to go drifting down, amusing himself with the strange sights while daylight lasted; but when night came, and the bridge to be passed, how then? Is it not better to be safe moored, though there be no beauty or variety in the scene?"

"Nay, Father, but is there no third way? Might the bridge not be passed in safety, and the child take his pleasure, and yet reach home well and sound?"

"Some children," said the Predicant Friar, with a tender intonation. "But not that child."

The Earl was silent. The Prior softly repeated a text of Scripture.

"'Endure chastisement. As sons God dealeth with

you; what son then is he, whom the Father chas-
teneth not ?"[1]

A low, half-repressed sigh from his companion
reminded the Prior that he was touching a sore
place. One of the Prince's bitterest griefs was his
childlessness.[2] The Prior tacked about, and came
into deeper water.

"'Nor have we a High Priest who cannot sym-
pathise with our infirmities, for He was tempted in
all things like us, except in sinning.'"[3]

"If one could see !" said the Earl, almost in a
whisper.

"It would be easier, without doubt. Yet 'blessed
are they who see not, and believe.' God can see.
I would rather He saw and not I, than—if such
a thing were possible — that I saw and not He.
Whether is better, my Lord, that the father see the
danger and guard the child without his knowing
anything, or that the child see it too, and have all
the pain and apprehension consequent upon the
seeing ? The blind has the advantage, sometimes."

"Yet who would wish to be blind on that account ?" answered the Earl, quickly.

"No man could wish it, nor need he. Only, the
blind man may take the comfort of it."

"But you have not answered one point, Father.
Why does God rouse longings in our hearts which
He never means to fulfil ?"

---

[1] Heb. xii. 7, Vulgate version.
[2] He has told us so himself.   [3] Heb. iv. 15, Vulgate version.

" Does God rouse them ? "

" Are they sin, then ? "

" No," answered the Prior, slowly, as if he were thinking out the question, and had barely reached the answer. " I dare not say that. They are nature. Some, I know, would have all that is nature to be sin; but I doubt if God treats it thus in His Word. Still, I question if He raises those longings. He allows them. Man raises them."

" Does He never guide them ? "

" Yes, that I think He does."

" Then the question comes to the same thing. Why does God not guide us to long for the thing that He means to give us ? "

" He very often does."

" Then," pursued the Earl, a little impatiently, " why does He not turn us away from that which He does not intend us to have ? "

" My Lord," said the Predicant, gravely, " from the day of his fall, man has always been asking God *why*. He will probably go on doing it to the day of the dissolution of all things. But I do not observe that God has ever yet answered the question."

" It is wrong to ask it, then, I suppose," said the Earl, with a weary sigh.

" It is not faith that wants to know why. 'He that believeth hasteneth not.' 'What I do, thou knowest not now; but thou shalt know hereafter."[2] We can afford to wait, my Lord."

[1] Isaiah xxviii. 16, Vulgate version.   [2] John xiii. 7

"Easily enough," replied the Earl, with feeling, "if we knew it would come right in the end."

"It will come as He would have it who laid down His life that you should live for ever. Is that not enough for my Lord?"

Perhaps the Prince felt it enough. At all events, he gave no answer.

"Well, that is not my notion of going comfortably through life!" observed Miss Elaine Criketot, in a decided tone. "My idea is to pull all the plums out of the cake, and leave the hard crusts for those that like them."

"Does anybody like them?" laughingly asked Clarice.

"Well, for those who need them, then. Plenty of folks in this world are glad of hard crusts or anything else."

"Thy metaphor is becoming rather confused," observed Diana.

"Dost thou not think, Elaine Criketot, that it might be only fair to leave a few plums for those whose usual fare is crusts? A crust now and then would scarcely hurt the dainty damsels who commonly regale themselves on plums."

It was a fourth voice which said this—a voice which nobody expected, and the sound of which brought all the girls to their feet in an instant.

"Most certainly, Lord Earl," replied Elaine, courtesying low; "but I hope they would be somebody else's plums than mine."

"I see," said the Earl, with that sparkle of fun in his eyes, which they all knew. "Self-denial is a holy and virtuous quality, to be cultivated by all men—except me. Well, we might all subscribe that creed with little sacrifice. But then where would be the self-denial?"

"Please it the Lord Earl, it might be practised by those who liked it."

"I should be happy to hear of any one who liked self-denial," responded the Earl, laughing. "Is that not a contradiction in terms?"

Elaine was about to make a half-saucy answer, mixed sufficiently with reverence to take away any appearance of offence, when a sight met her eyes which struck her into silent horror. In the door-way, looking a shade more acetous than usual, stood Lady Margaret. It was well known to all the bower-maidens of the Countess of Cornwall that there were two crimes on her code which were treated as capital offences. Laughing was the less, and being caught in conversation with a man was the greater. But beneath both these depths was a deeper depth yet, and this was talking to the Earl. Never was a more perfect exemplification of the dog in the manger than the Lady Margaret of Cornwall. She did not want the Earl for herself, but she was absolutely determined that no one else should so much as speak to him. Here was Elaine, caught red-handed in the commission of all three of these stupendous crimes. And if the offence could be made worse, it was so by the Earl saying, as he walked away, "I pray you, my Lady, visit not my sins on this young maid."

Had one compassionate sensation remained in the mind of the Countess towards Elaine, that unlucky speech would have extinguished it at once. She did not, as usual, condescend to answer her lord; but she turned to Elaine, and in a voice of concentrated anger, demanded the repetition of every word which had passed. Diana gave it, for Elaine seemed almost paralysed with terror. Clarice, on the demand of her mistress, confirmed Diana's report as exact. The Countess turned back to Elaine. Her words were scarcely to be reported, for she lost alike her temper and her gentlewomanly manners. "And out of my house thou goest this day," was the conclusion, "thou shameful, giglot hussey! And I will not give thee an husband; thou shalt go back to thy father and thy mother, with the best whipping that ever I gave maid. And she that shall be in thy stead shall be the ugliest maid I can find, and still of tongue, and sober of behaviour. Now, get thee gone!"

And calling for Agatha as she went, the irate lady stalked away.

Of no use was poor Elaine's flood of tears, nor the united entreaties of her four companions. Clarice and Diana soon found that they were not to come off scatheless. Neither had spoken to the Earl, as Elaine readily confessed; but for the offence of listening to such treachery, both were sent to bed by daylight, with bread and water for supper. The offences of grown-up girls in those days were punished like those of little children now. All took tearful farewells of poor Elaine, who dolefully expressed her fear of another whipping when she reached home; and so she passed out of their life.

It was several weeks before the new bower-maiden appeared. Diana suggested that the Countess found some difficulty in meeting with a girl ugly enough to please her. But, at last, one evening in November, Mistress Underdone introduced the new-comer, in the person of a girl of eighteen, or thereabouts, as Felicia de Fay, daughter of Sir Stephen de Fay and Dame Sabina Watefeud, of the county of Sussex All the rest looked with much curiosity at her.

Felicia, while not absolutely ugly, was undeniably plain. Diana remarked afterwards to Clarice that there were no ugly girls to be had, as plainly appeared. But the one thing about her which really was ugly was her expression. She looked no one in the face, while she diligently studied every one who was not looking at her. Let any one attempt to meet her eyes, and they dropped in a moment Some do this from mere bashfulness, but Felicia showed no bashfulness in any other way. Clarice's feeling towards her was fear.

"I'm not afraid!" said Diana. "I am sure I could be her match in fair fight!"

"It is the fair fight I doubt," said Clarice. "I am afraid there is treachery in her eyes."

"She makes me creep all over," added Olympias.

"Well, she had better not try to measure swords with me," said Diana. "I tell you, I have a presentiment that girl and I shall fight; but I will come off victor; you see if I don't!"

Clarice made no answer, but in her heart she thought that Diana was too honest to be any match for Felicia.

It was the Countess's custom to spend her afternoon, when the day was fine, in visiting some shrine or abbey. When the day was not fine, she passed the time in embroidering among her maidens, and woe betide the unlucky damsel who selected a wrong shade, or set in a false stitch. The natural result of this was that the pine-cone, kept by Olympias as a private barometer, was anxiously consulted on the least appearance of clouds. Diana asserted that she offered a wax candle to St. Wulstan every month for fair weather. One of the young ladies always had to accompany her mistress, and the fervent hope of each was to escape this promotion. Felicia alone never expressed this hope, never joined in any tirades against the Countess, never got into disgrace with her, and seemed to stand alone, like a drop of vinegar which would not mingle with the oil around it. She appeared to see everything, and say nothing. It was impossible to get at her likes and dislikes. She took everything exactly alike. Either she had no prejudices, or she was all prejudice, and nobody could tell which it was.

CHAPTER V.

BUILDING A FRESH CASTLE.

"Oh, had I wist, afore I kissed,
    That loue had been sae ill to win,
I'd locked my heart wi' a key o' gowd,
    And pinned it wi' a siller pin."—*Old Ballad.*

N an afternoon early in December, the Countess sat among her bower-women at work. Roisia was almost in tears, for she had just been sharply chidden for choosing too pale a shade of blue. A little stir at the door made all look up, and they saw Father Bevis. All rose to their feet in an instant, the Countess dropping on her knees, and entreating the priest's blessing. He gave it, but as if his thoughts were far away.

"Lady, my Lord hath sent me to you with tidings. May God grant they be not the worst tidings for England that we have heard for many a day! A messenger is come from the North, bringing news that the Lady Alianora the Queen lieth dead in the marsh lands of Lincolnshire."

It was a worse loss to England than any there knew. Yet they knew enough to draw a cry of horror and sorrow from the lips of all those that heard the news. And a fortnight later, on the 17th of December, they all stood at Charing Cross, to see the funeral procession wind down from the north road, and set down the black bier for its last momentary rest on the way to Westminster.

It is rather singular that the two items which alone the general reader usually remembers of this good Queen's history should be two points distinctly proved by research to be untrue. Leonor did not suck the poison from her husband's arm—a statement never made until a hundred and fifty years after her death, and virtually disproved by the testimony of an eye-witness who makes no allusion to it, but who tells us instead that she behaved like a very weak woman instead of a very brave one, giving way to hysterical screams, and so distressing the sufferer that he bade four of his knights to carry her out of the room. Again, Edward's affectionate regret did not cause the erection of the famous Eleanor Crosses wherever the bier rested on its journey. Leonor herself desired their erection, and left money for it in her will.

The domestic peace of the royal house died with her who had stood at its head for nineteen years. To her son, above all others, her loss was simply irreparable. The father and son were men of very different tastes and proclivities ; and the former never understood the latter. In fact, Edward II. was a man who did not belong to his century; and such men always have a hard lot. His love of quiet, and hatred of war, were, in the eyes of his father, spirit-less meanness ; while his musical tastes and his love of animals went beyond womanish weakness, and were looked upon as absolute vices. But perhaps to the nobles the worst features of his character were two which, in the nineteenth century, would entitle him to respect. He was extremely faithful in friend-ship, and he had a strong impatience of etiquette. He loved to associate with his people, to mix in their joys and sorrows, to be as one of them. His favour-ite amusement was to row down the Thames on a summer evening, with music on board, and to chat freely with the lieges who came down in their barges, occasionally, and much to his own amuse-ment, buying cabbages and other wares from them. We should consider such actions indicative of a kindly disposition and of simplicity of taste. But in the eyes of his contemporaries they were inexpres-sibly low. And be it remembered that it was not a question of associating with persons of more or less education, whose mental standard might be un-equal to his own. There was no mental standard whereby to measure any one in the thirteenth cen-tury. All (with a very few exceptions, and those chiefly among the clergy) were uneducated alike. The moral standard looked upon war and politics as the only occupations meet for a prince, and upon hunting and falconry as the only amusements suffi-ciently noble. A man who, like Edward, hated war, and had no fancy for either sport or politics,

F

was hardly a man in the eyes of a mediæval noble.

The hardest treatment to which Edward was subjected, whether from his father in youth or from his people at a later time, arose out of that touching constancy which was his greatest virtue. Perhaps he did not always choose his friends well; he was inclined to put rather too much trust in his fellow-creatures; and Hugh Le Despenser the elder may have been grasping and mean, and Piers Gavestone too extravagant. Yet we must remember that we read their characters only as depicted by the pens of men who hated them—of men who were simply unable to conceive that two persons might be drawn together by mutual taste for some elevated and innocent pursuit. The most wicked motives imaginable were recklessly suggested for the attachment which Edward showed for these chosen friends—who were not of noble origin, and had no handles to their names till he conferred them.

It is only through a thick mist of ignorance and prejudice that we of this day can see the character of Edward II. We read it only in the pages of monks who hated their Lollard King—in the angry complaints of nobles who were jealous that he listened to and bestowed gifts on other men than themselves. But we do see some faint glimpses of the Edward that really was, in the letter-book but recently dug out of a mass of State papers; in the pages of De La Moor,[1] the only chronicler of his deeds who did not hate him, and who, as his personal attendant, must have known more of him in a month than the monks could have learned in a century; and last, not least, in that touching Latin poem in which, during the sad captivity which preceded his sadder death, he poured out his soul to God, the only Friend whom he had left in all the universe.

> "Oh, who that heard how once they praised my name,
> Could think that from those tongues these slanders came?
> . . . I see Thy rod, and, Lord, I am content.
> Weave Thou my life until the web is spun;
> Chide me, O Father, till Thy will be done:
> Thy child no longer murmurs to obey;
> He only sorrows o'er the past delay.
> Lost is my realm; yet I shall not repine,
> If, after all, I win but that of Thine."[2]

To a character such as this, the loss of his chief friend and only reliable intercessor, when just emerging from infancy into boyhood, was a loss for which nothing could atone. It proved itself so in those dreary after-years of perpetual misunderstandings and severities on the part of his father, who set him no good example, and yet looked on the son whose tastes were purer than his own as an instance of irredeemable depravity. The easiest thing in the world to do is one against which God has denounced a woe —to put bitter for sweet, and sweet for bitter.

---

[1] De La Moor is the only chronicler in whose pages it is possible to recognise the Edward of the letter-book, in which all his letters are copied for the thirty-third year of his father's reign—1304-5.

[2] Barnes's Edward III. I must in honesty confess that I have taken the liberty of smoothing Dr. Barnes's somewhat rugged translation.

Another item of sorrowful news reached London with the coffin of Queen Leonor. It was the death of the baby Queen of Scotland, by whose betrothal to Prince Edward the King had vainly hoped to fuse the northern and southern kingdoms into one. It left Scotland in a condition of utter distraction, with no less than eleven different claimants for the Crown, setting up claims good, bad, and indifferent; but every one of them persuaded that all the others had not an inch of ground to stand on, and that he was the sole true and rightful inheritor.

The only claimants who really had a shadow of right may be reduced to three. If the old primitive custom of Scotland was to be regarded—a custom dear to all Celtic nations—by which illegitimate children were considered to have an equal right to the succession with the legitimate ones, then there could be no question that the heir was Patrick de Galithlys, son of Henry, the natural son of Alexander II. But if not—and in this respect undoubtedly the custom had become obsolete—the struggle rested between John Baliol and Robert Bruce, of whom the first was the son of Dervorgoyl, daughter of Margaret, eldest daughter of David Earl of Huntingdon, brother of King William the Lion; while the latter was the son of Isabel, the second daughter of David. Every reader knows that the question was submitted by consent of the Scottish nobles to Edward I. as arbitrator, and that he gave his decision in favour of Baliol. In other words, he gave it against the existing law both of England and Scotland, which did not recognise representation, and according to which the son of the second sister ought to have been preferred to the grandson of the elder.

The anxiety of our kings to bring in this law of representation is a curious psychological fact. Richard I. tried to do it by will, in leaving the crown to his nephew Arthur; but the law was too strong for him, and the rightful heir succeeded—his brother John. Edward I. contrived to abrogate the law, so far as Scotland was concerned, a hundred years later. And eighty years after him Edward III. tried again to alter the English law of succession, and this time the experiment succeeded. But its success was due mainly to two reasons—the personal popularity of the dead Prince whose son was thus lifted into the line of succession, while the rightful heir was extremely unpopular; and the fact that the disinherited heir gave full consent and assistance to the change in the law.

The knights and squires of the Earl of Cornwall's household were gathered together on the balcony which faced the river. One only was absent, Piers Ingham, who was occupied in a more interesting manner, as will presently be seen. His colleague, Sir Lambert Aylmer, was holding forth in a lively manner for the benefit of the four squires, who were listening to him with various degrees of attention.

Reginald de Echingham could never spare much of that quality from his admirable self, and De Chaucombe was an original thinker, who did not purchase ready-made ideas from other people. Barkeworth invariably agreed with the last speaker in public, but kept his private views an inscrutable mystery; while all that could be said of Gernet's notions was that he had *" un grand talent pour le silence."*

To this quartette Sir Lambert was explaining his forecast of the political weather. The young knight had a great fancy for airing his politics, and an unwavering conviction of the infallibility of his judgment. If Sir Lambert was to be believed, what King Edward would undoubtedly do was to foment civil war in Scotland, until all the rival male claimants had destroyed each other. He would then marry the daughter of one of them, and annex Scotland as her appanage. All being smooth in that quarter, the King would next undertake a pilgrimage to Palestine, drive the Saracens out, and confer that country on one of his sons-in-law. He would then carry fire and sword through Borussia, Lithuania, and other heathen kingdoms in the north, subdue them all, put a few more sons-in-law in possession as tributary governors, and being by that time an old man, would then return to Westminster to end his days in peace, a new Alexander, and to leave a magnificent empire to his son.

" Easier said than done," growled De Chaucombe, in his beard.

"Charming!" observed De Echingham, caressing his pet moustache.

"A lovely prospect, indeed," said De Barkeworth, with a bow, in a tone so impartially suspended between conviction and cynicism that nobody could tell which had dictated it. "I should like to win my spurs in Lithuania."

"Win thy spurs!" muttered De Chaucombe again. "There are no spurs for carpet-knights[1] in the wardrobe of the Future."

"I think knights should have golden spurs, not gilt ones—don't you?" inquired De Echingham.

"Puppy!" sneered De Chaucombe. "If ever either are on thy heels it will be a blunder of somebody's making."

"Is it necessary to quarrel?" asked Gernet, speaking for the first time.

"Oh, I trust I have more generosity than to quarrel with *him*," rather contemptuously returned De Echingham, who, as every one present knew, had as little physical courage as any girl.

"Make thyself easy," was the answer of De Chaucombe, as he walked away. "I should not think of running the risk."

"What risk?" demanded Barkeworth, laughing.

De Chaucombe looked back over his shoulder, and discharged a Parthian dart.

[1] A carpet-knight was one whose heroism lay more in rhetorical visions addressed to his partner in the intervals of dancing than in hard blows given and taken in the field.

"The risk of turning my good Damascus blade on a toad," said he, to the great amusement of Barkeworth.

De Chaucombe went to the end of the balcony, descended the steps which led to the ground floor, and came on a second terrace, also fronting the river. As he turned a corner of the house he suddenly confronted two people, who were walking slowly along the terrace, and conversing in hushed tones. Sir Piers Ingham was evidently and deeply interested, his head slightly bowed towards Clarice who was as earnestly engaged in the dissection of one of the few leaves which Christmas had left fluttering on the garden bushes. As De Chaucombe approached she looked up with a startled air, and blushed to her eyes.

De Chaucombe muttered something indistinct which might pass for "Good evening," and resumed his path rather more rapidly than before.

"So the wind blows from that direction!" he said to himself. "Well, it does not matter a straw to me. But what our amiable mistress will say to the fair Clarice, when she comes to know of it, is another question. I do believe that, if she had made up her mind to a match between them, she would undo it again, if she thought they wished it. It would be just like her."

It had never occurred to Clarice to suppose that she did anything wrong in thus disobeying point blank the known orders of her mistress that the

bower-maidens were to hold no intercourse whatever with the gentlemen of the household. She
knew perfectly well that if the Countess saw her
talking to Sir Piers, she would be exceedingly
angry; and she knew that her parents fully intended and expected her to obey her mistress as
she would themselves. Poor Clarice's code of morals
looked upon discovery, not disobedience, as the
thing to be dreaded; and while she would have
recoiled with horror from the thought of unfaithful-
ness to her beloved, she looked with absolute com-
placency on the idea of disloyalty to the mistress
whom she by no means loved. How could she
do otherwise when she had never been taught
better?

Clarice's standard was *loyauté d'amour*. It is the
natural standard of all men, the only difference being
in the king whom they set up. A vast number are
loyal to themselves only, for it is themselves whom
alone they love. Fewer are loyal to some human
being; and poor humanity being a very fallible
thing, they often make sad shipwreck. Very few
indeed—in comparison of the mass—are loyal to
the King who claims and has a right to their hearts'
best affections. And Clarice was not one of these.

Inside the house the Countess and Mistress
Underdone were very busy indeed. Before them,
spread over forms and screens, lay piles of material
for clothing—linen, serge, silk, and crape, of many
colours. On a leaf-table at the side of the room

a number of gold and silver ornaments were dis-
played. Furs were heaped upon the bed, boots and
loose slippers stood in a row in one corner; while
Mistress Underdone was turning over for her mistress's inspection a quantity of embroidered necker-
chiefs.

"Now, let me see," said the Countess, peremp-
torily. "Measure off linen for four gowns, Agatha
—two of brown and two of red. Serge for two—
the dark green. One silk will be enough, and one
of crape."

"How many ells the gown does my Lady choose
to allow?" asked Mistress Underdone, taking an
ell-wand from the table.

"Four," said the Countess, curtly. This was
rather miserly measure, four ells and a third being
the usual reckoning; but Mistress Underdone measured and cut in silence.

"Thou mayest allow a third more for the silk
and crape," said the Countess, in a fit of unusual
generosity.

Mistress Underdone finished her measuring, laying
each piece of material neatly folded on the last,
until the table held a tall heap of them.

"Now for hoods," pursued the Countess. "Black
cloth for two, lined with cats' fur; russet for two
more. Capes for outdoor wear—two of the green
serge; one of black cloth lined with cats' fur; one
of silk. Four linen wimples; two pairs of cloth
boots, two of slippers; two corsets; three of those

broidered kerchiefs, one better than the others ; four
pairs of hosen. Measure off also twenty-four ells
of linen cloth."

"Of what price, if it please my Lady?"

"Fivepence the ell. And the boots of sixpence
a pair. What did that green serge cost?"

"Threepence the ell, my Lady."

"That is monstrous. Have I no cheaper? Twopence would be good enough for her."

"If it please my Lady, there is only that coarse
grey serge at three halfpence the ell, which was
bought for the cookmaids."

"Humph! I suppose that would scarcely do," said
the Countess, in a tone which sounded as if she
wished it would. "Well, then—those ornaments. She
must have a silver fibula, I suppose; and a copper-
gilt one for common. What made thee put out all
those other things? That is enough for her. If she
wants a silver chain, her husband must give it her;
I shall not. As to rings and necklaces, they are all
nonsense—not fit for such as she."

"Would my Lady think proper to allow a dovecote
with silver pins?"

The dovecote was a head-dress, a kind of round
caul of gold or silver network, secured by gold or
silver pins fastened in the hair.

"Not I. Let her husband give her such fooleries."

"And may I request to know what my Lady allows
for making the garments?"

"Three halfpence each."

"Might I be pardoned if I remind my Lady that
the usual price is twopence each?"

"For me, perhaps; not for her."

Mistress Underdone went on measuring the linen
in silence.

"There, that finishes for Clarice," said the
Countess. "Now for Diana. She may have a silver
chain in addition, two of the best kerchiefs, and—no,
that is enough. Otherwise let her have just the
same."

"If my Lady would graciously indulge her servant
with permission to ask it, do the maidens know yet
what is to befall them?"

"No. I shall tell them on Sunday. Time enough."

And the Countess left Mistress Underdone to finish
the work by herself.

"On Sunday! Only two days beforehand!" said
Agatha Underdone to herself. "Diana will stand it.
She is one that would not care much for anything of
that kind, and she will rule the house. But Clarice!
If she should have given her heart elsewhere!—and I
have fancied, lately, that she has given it somewhere.
That poor child!"

"But how can we?" queried Clarice. "If I were to
speak to the Lady—even if I dared—I doubt——"

"I do not doubt, sweetheart," replied Sir Piers.
"No, the path must be rather more winding than
that, though I confess I hate tortuous paths. Father
Miles is the only person who has any influence with

the Lady, and Father Bevis is the only one who has any with him."

" But Father Bevis would have no sympathy with a love-story."

" I am not sure that he would. But my Lord will, I know ; and Father Bevis will listen to him. Leave this business to me, my fair Clarice. If I can obtain my Lord's ear this evening after vespers, and I think I can, we shall soon have matters in train ; and I have a fine hawk for Father Miles, which will put him in a good humour. Now, farewell, for I hear the Lady's voice within."

The lovers parted hastily, and Clarice went in to attire herself for mass. For any one of her maidens to be absent from that ceremony would have been a terrible offence in the eyes of the Countess ; nor would any less excuse than serious illness have availed to avert her displeasure. Dinner followed mass, and a visit to the shrine of St. Edward, concluded by vespers, occupied the remainder of the afternoon. There was half an hour to spare before supper, and the girls were chatting together in their usual " bower," or boudoir, when, to their surprise, the Countess entered.

" I have ado but with two of you," she said, as she seated herself.

Naturally, the girls supposed that some penalty was about to befall those two. How had they offended her? and which of them were the offenders ? To displease the Countess, as they all knew, was so extremely easy, that not one of them was prepared for the next sentence.

"Two of you are to be wed on Tuesday."

This was a bombshell. And it was the more serious because they were aware that from this sentence there was no appeal. Troubled eyes, set in white faces, hurriedly sought each other.

Was it from sheer thoughtlessness, or from absolute malice, or even from a momentary feeling of compassion towards the two who were to be sacrificed, that the Countess made a long pause after each sentence ?

"Diana Quappelad," she said.

Olympias, Roisia, and Clarice drew a sigh of relief. There were just half the chances against each that there had been. Diana stood forward, with a slight flush, but apparently not much concerned.

"Thou art to wed with Master Fulk de Chaucombe, and thy bridegroom will be knighted on the wedding-day. I shall give thee thy gear and thy wedding-feast. Mistress Underdone will show thee the gear."

The first momentary expression of Diana's face had been disappointment. It passed in an instant, and one succeeded which was divided between pleasurable excitement and amusement. She courtesied very low, and thanked the Countess, as of course was expected of her.

Roisia stood behind, with blank face and clasped hands. There might be further pain in store, but pleasure for her there could now be none. The Countess quite understood the dumb show, but she made no sign.

" Clarice La Theyn."

The girl stood out, listening for the next words as though her life hung on them.

" I shall also give thee thy gear, and thy squire will be knighted on the wedding-day."

The Countess was turning away as though she had said all. Clarice had heard enough to make her feel as if life were not worth having. A squire who still required knighthood was not Piers Ingham. Did it matter who else it was? But she found, the next moment, that it might.

" Would my Lady suffer me to let Clarice know whom she is to wed ?" gently suggested Mistress Underdone.

" Oh, did I not mention it ? " carelessly responded the Countess, turning back to Clarice. "Vivian Barkeworth."

She paused an instant for the courtesy and thanks which she expected. But she got a good deal more than she expected. With a passionate sob that came from her very heart, Clarice fell at the feet of the Lady Margaret.

" What is all this fuss about ?" exclaimed her displeased mistress. " I never heard such ado about nothing."

Her displeasure, usually feared above all things, was nothing to Clarice in that terrible instant. She sobbed forth that she loved elsewhere—she was already trothplight.

"Nonsense!" said the Countess, sharply. "What business hadst thou with such foolery, unknown to me? All maidens are wed by orders from their superiors. Why shouldst thou be an exception?"

"Oh, have you no compassion?" cried poor Clarice, in her agony. "Lady, did you never love?"

All present were intently watching the face of the Countess, in the hope of seeing some sign of relenting. But when this question was asked, the stern lips grew more set and stern than ever, and something like fire flashed out of the usually cold blue-grey eyes.

"Who—I?" she exclaimed. "Thanks be to all the saints right verily, nay. I never had ado with any such disgraceful folly. From mine earliest years I have ever desired to be an holy sister, and never to see a man's face. Get up, girl; it is of no use to kneel to me. There was no kindness shown to me; my wishes were never considered; why should thine be? I was made to array myself for my bridal, to the very uprooting and destruction of all that I most loved and desired. Ah! if my Lord and father had lived, it would not have been so; he always encouraged my vocation. He said love was unhappy, and I thought it was scandalous. No, Clarice; I have no compassion upon lovers. There never ought to be any such thing. Let it be as I have said."

And away stalked the Countess, looking more grey, square, and angular than ever.

CHAPTER VI.

DESTROYED BY THE HURRICANE.

"Our plans may be disjointed,
But we may calmly rest :
What God has once appointed
Is better than our best."
—FRANCES RIDLEY HAVERGAL.

THE Countess left Clarice prostrate on the ground, sobbing as if her heart would break—Olympias feebly trying to raise and soothe her, Roisia looking half-stunned, and Felicia palpably amused by the scene.

"Thou hadst better get up, child," said Diana, in a tone divided between constraint and pity. "It will do thee no good to lie there. We shall all have to put up with the same thing in our turn. I haven't got the man I should have chosen; but I suppose it won't matter a hundred years hence."

"I am not so sure of that," said Roisia, in a low voice.

"Oh, thou art disappointed, I know," said Diana. "I would hand Fulk over to thee with pleasure, if I could. I don't want him. But I suppose he will

G

do as well as another, and I shall take care to be mistress. It is something to be married—to anybody."

"It is everything to be married to the right man," said Roisia; "but it is something very awful to be married to the wrong one."

"Oh, one soon gets over that," was Diana's answer. "So long as you can have your own way, I don't see that anything signifies much. I shall not admire myself in my wedding-dress any the less because my squire is not exactly the one I hoped it might be."

"Diana, I don't understand thee," responded Roisia. "What does it matter, I should say, having thine own way in little nothings so long as thou art not to have it in the one thing for which thou really carest? Thou dost not mean to say that a velvet gown would console thee for breaking thy heart?"

"But I do," said Diana. "I must be a countess before I could wear velvet; and I would marry any man in the world who would make me a countess."

Mistress Underdone, who had lifted up Clarice, and was holding her in her arms, petting her into calmness as she would a baby, now thought fit to interpose.

"My maids," she said, "there are women who have lost their hearts, and there are women who were born without any. The former case has the more suffering, yet methinks the latter is really the more pitiable."

"Well, I think those people pitiable enough who let their hearts break their sleep and interfere with their appetites," replied Diana. "I have got over my disappointment already; and Clarice will be a simpleton if she do not."

"I expect Clarice and I will be simpletons," said Roisia, quietly.

"Please yourselves, and I will please myself," answered Diana. "Now, mistress, Clarice seems to have given over crying for a few seconds; may we see the gear?"

"Oh, I want Father Bevis!" sobbed Clarice, with a fresh gush of tears.

"Ay, my dove, thou wilt be the better of shriving," said Mistress Underdone, tenderly. "Sit thee down a moment, and I will see to Father Bevis. Wait awhile, Diana."

It was not many minutes before she came back with Father Bevis, who took Clarice into his oratory; and as it was a long while before she rejoined them, the others—Roisia excepted—had almost time to forget the scene they had witnessed, in the interest of turning over Diana's *trousseau,* and watching her try on hoods and mantles.

The interview with Father Bevis was unsatisfactory to Clarice. She wanted comfort, and he gave her none. Advice he was ready with in plenty; but comfort he could not give her, because he could not see why she wanted it. He was simply incapable of understanding her. He was very kind, and very anxious to comfort her, if he could only have told how to do it. But love — spiritual love excepted—was a stranger to his bosom. No one had ever loved him; he could not remember his parents; he had never had brother nor sister; and he had never made a friend. His heart was there, but it had never been warmed to life. Perhaps he came nearest to loving the Earl his master; but even this feeling awakened very faint pulsations. His capacity for loving human beings had been simply starved to death. Such a man as this, however anxious to be kind and helpful, of course could not enter in the least into the position of Clarice. He told her many very true things, if she had been capable of receiving them; he tried his very best to help her; but she felt through it all that they were barbarians to each other, and that Father Bevis regarded her as partially incomprehensible and wholly silly.

Father Bevis told Clarice that the chief end of man was to glorify God, and to enjoy Him for ever; that no love was worthy in comparison with His; that he who loved father and mother more than Christ was not worthy of Him. All very true, but the stunned brain and lacerated heart could not take it in. The drugs were pure and precious, but they were not the medicine for her complaint. She only felt a sensation of repulsion.

Clarice did not know that the Earl was doing his very best to rescue her. He insisted on Father Miles going to the Countess about it; nay, he even ventured an appeal to her himself, though it always cost him great pain to attempt a conversation with this beloved but irresponsive woman. But he took nothing by his motion. The Countess was as obstinate as she was absolute. If anything, the opposition to her will left her just a shade more determined. In vain her husband pleaded earnestly with her not to spoil two lives. Hers had been spoiled, she replied candidly: these ought not to be better off, nor should they be.

"Life has been spoiled for us both," said the Earl, sadly; "but I should have thought that a reason why we might have been tenderer to others."

"You are a fool!" said the Countess with a flash of angry scorn.

They were the first words she had spoken to him for eighteen years.

"Maybe, my Lady," was the gentle answer. "It would cost me less to be accounted a fool than it would to break a heart."

And he left her, feeling himself baffled and his endeavours useless, yet with a glow at his heart notwithstanding. His Margaret had spoken to him at last. That her words were angry, even abusive, was a consideration lost in the larger fact. Tears which did not fall welled up from the soft heart to the dove-like eyes, and he went out to the terrace to compose himself. "O Margaret, Margaret! if you could have loved me!" He never thought of blaming her—only of winning her. as a dim hope of some happy future, to be realised when it was God's will. He had never yet dared to look his cross in the face sufficiently to add, if it were God's will.

When the Monday came, which was to be the last day of Clarice's maiden life, it proved a busy, bustling day, with no time for thought until the evening. Clarice lived through it as best she might. Diana seemed to have put her disappointment completely behind her, and to be thoroughly consoled by the bustle and her *trousseau.*

One consideration never occurred to any of the parties concerned, which would be thought rather desirable in the nineteenth century. This was, that the respective bridegrooms should have any interview with their brides elect, or in the slightest degree endeavour to make themselves agreeable. They met at meals in the great hall, but they never exchanged a word. Clarice did not dare to lift her eyes, lest she should meet those either of Vivian or Piers. She kept them diligently fixed upon her trencher, with which she did little else than look at it.

The evening brought a lull in the excitement and busy labour. The Countess, attended by Felicia, had gone to the Palace on royal invitation. Clarice sat on the terrace, her eyes fixed on the river which she did not see, her hands lying listlessly in her lap. Though she had heard nothing, that unaccountable conviction of another presence, which comes to us all at times, seized upon her; and she looked up to see Piers Ingham.

The interview was long, and there is no need to add that it was painful. The end came at last.

"Wilt thou forget me, Clarice?" softly asked Piers.

"I ought," was the answer, with a gush of tears, "if I can."

"I cannot," was the reply. "But one pain I can spare thee, my beloved. The Lady means to retain thee in her service as damsel of the chamber."[1]

If Clarice could have felt any lesser grief beside the one great one, she would have been sorry to hear that.

"I shall retire," said Sir Piers, "from my Lord's household. I will not give thee the misery of meeting me day by day. Rather I will do what I can to help thee to forget me. It is the easier for me, since I have had to offend my Lady by declining the hand of Felicia de Fay, which she was pleased to offer me."

"The Lady offered Felicia to thee?"

Sir Piers bent his head in assent. Clarice felt as if she could have poisoned Felicia, and have given what arsenic remained over to the Lady Margaret.

---

[1] There were two divisions of "damsels" in the household of a mediæval princess, the *domicella* and the *domicella cameræ.* The former, who corresponded to the modern Maids of Honour, were young and unmarried ; the latter, the Ladies of the Bedchamber, were always married women. Sufficient notice of this distinction has not been taken by modern writers. Had it so been, the supposition long held of the identity of Philippa Chaucer, *domicella cameræ,* with Philippa Pycard, *domicella,* could scarcely have arisen ; nor should we be told that Chaucer's marriage did not occur until 1369, or later, when we find Philippa in office as Lady of the Bedchamber in 1366.

"And are we never to meet again?" she asked, with an intonation of passionate sorrow.

"That must depend on God's will," said Sir Piers, gravely.

Clarice covered her face with both hands, and the bitter tears trickled fast through her fingers.

"Oh, why is God's will so hard?" she cried. "Could He not have left us in peace? We had only each other."

"Hush, sweet heart! It is wrong to say that. And yet it is hardly possible not to think it."

"It is not possible!" sobbed Clarice. "Does not God know it is not possible?"

"I suppose He must," said Sir Piers, gloomily.

There was no comfort in the thought to either. There never is any to those who do not know God. And Piers was only feeling after Him, if haply he might find Him, and barely conscious even of that; while Clarice had not reached even that point. To both of them, in this very anguish, Christ was saying, "Come unto Me;" but their own cry of pain hindered them from hearing Him. It was not likely they should hear, just then, when the sunlight of life was being extinguished, and the music was dying to its close. But afterwards, in the silence and the darkness, when the sounds were hushed and the lights were out, and there was nothing that could be done but to endure, then the still, small voice might make itself heard, and the crushed hearts might sob out their answer.

So they parted. "They took but ane kiss, and tare themselves away," to meet when it was God's will, and not knowing on which side of the river of death that would be.

Half an hour had passed since Sir Piers' step had died away on the terrace, and Clarice still sat where he had left her, in crushed and silent stillness. If this night could only be the end of it! If things had not to go on!

"Clarice," said a pitying voice; and a hand was laid upon her head as if in fatherly blessing.

Clarice was too stunned with pain to remember her courtly duties. She only looked up at Earl Edmund.

"Clarice, my poor child! I want thee to know that I did my best for thee."

"I humbly thank your Lordship," Clarice forced herself to say.

"And it may be, my child, though it seems hard to believe, that God is doing His best for thee too."

"Then what would His worst be?" came in a gush from Clarice.

"It might be that for which thou wouldst thank Him now."

The sorrowing girl was arrested in spite of herself, for the Earl spoke in that tone of quiet certainty which has more effect on an undecided mind than any words. She wondered how he knew, not realising that he knows "more than the ancients" who knows God and sorrow.

"My child," said the Earl again, "man's best and God's best are often very different things. In the eyes of Monseigneur Saint Jacob, the best thing would have been to spare his son from being cast into the pit and sold to the Ishmaelites. But God's best was to sell the boy into slavery, and to send him into a dungeon, and then to lift him up to the steps of the king's throne. When *then* comes, Clarice, we shall be satisfied with what happened to us now."

"When will it come, my Lord?" asked Clarice, in a dreary tone.

"When it is best," replied the Earl quietly.

"Your Lordship speaks as if you knew!" said Clarice.

"God knows. And he who knows God may be sure of everything else."

"Is it so much to know God?"

"It is life. 'Without God' and 'Without hope' are convertible terms."

"My Lord," said Clarice, wondering much to hear a layman use language which it seemed to her was only fit for priests, "how may one know God?"

"Go and ask Him. How dost thou know any one? Is it not by converse and companionship?"

There was a silent pause till the Earl spoke again.

"Clarice," he said, "our Lord has a lesson to teach thee. It rests with thee to learn it well or ill. If thou choose to be idle and obstinate, and refuse to learn, thou mayest sit all day long on the form in disgrace, and only have the task perfect at last when thou art wearied out with thine own perverseness. But if thou take the book willingly, and apply thyself with heart and mind, the task will be soon over, and the teacher may give thee leave to go out into the sunshine."

"My Lord," said Clarice, "I do not know how to apply your words here. How can I learn this task quickly?"

"Dost thou know, first, what the task is?"

"Truly, no."

"Then let a brother tell thee who has had it set to him. It is a hard lesson, Clarice, and one that an inattentive scholar can make yet harder if he will. It is, 'Not my will, but Thine, be done.'"

"I cannot! I cannot!" cried Clarice passionately.

"Some scholars say that," replied the Earl gently, "until the evening shadows grow very long. They are the weariest of all when they reach home."

"My Lord, pardon me, but you cannot understand it!" Clarice stood up. "I am young, and you——"

"I am over forty years," replied the Earl. "Ah, child, dost thou make that blunder?—dost thou think the child's sorrows worse than the man's? I have known both, and I tell thee the one is not to be compared to the other. Young hearts are apt to think it, for grief is a thing new and strange to them. But if ever it become to thee as thy daily bread, thou wilt understand it better. It has been mine, Clarice, for eighteen years."

That was a year more than Clarice had been in the world. She looked up wonderingly into the saddened, dove-like Plantagenet eyes—those eyes characteristic of the House—so sweet in repose, so fiery in anger. Clarice had but a dim idea what his sorrow was.

"My Lord," she said, half inquiringly, "methinks you never knew such a grief as mine?"

The smile which parted the Earl's lips was full of pity.

"Say rather, maiden, that thou never knewest one like mine. But God knows both, Clarice, and He pities both, and when His time comes He will comfort both. At the best time, child! Only let us acquaint ourselves with Him, for so only can we be at peace. And now, farewell. I had better go in and preach my sermon to myself."

Clarice was left alone again. She did not turn back to exactly the same train of thought. A new idea had been given her, which was to become the germ of a long train of others. She hardly put it into words, even to herself; but it was this—that God meant something. He was not sitting on the throne of the universe in placid indifference to her sorrows; neither was He a malevolent Being who delighted in interfering with the plans of His creatures simply to exhibit His own power. He was doing this—somehow—for her benefit. She saw neither the how nor the why; but He saw them, and He meant good to her. All the world was not limited to the Slough of Despond at her feet. There was blue sky above.

Very vaguely Clarice realised this. But it was sufficient to soften the rocky hardness which had been the worst element of her pain—to take away the blind chance against which her impotent wings had been beaten in vain efforts to escape from the dark cage. It was that contact with "the living will of a living person," which gives the human element to what would otherwise be hard, blind, pitiless fate.

Clarice rose, and looked up to the stars. No words came. The cry of her heart was, "O Lord, I am oppressed; undertake for me." But she was too ignorant to weave it into a prayer. When human hearts look up to God in wordless agony, the Intercessor translates the attitude into the words of Heaven.

Sad or bright, there was no time for thought on the Tuesday morning. The day was bitterly cold, for it was the 16th of January 1291, and a heavy hoar-frost silvered all the trees, and weighed down the bushes in the Palace garden. Diana, wrapped in her white furs, was the picture of health and merriment. Was it because she really had not enough heart to care, or because she was determined not to give herself a moment to consider? Clarice, white as the fur round her throat, pale and heavy-eyed, grave and silent, followed Diana into the Palace chapel. The Countess was there, handsomely attired, and the Earl, in golden armour; but they stood on opposite sides of the chancel, and the former ignored her lord's existence. Diana's wedding came first. De Chaucombe behaved a. little more amiably than usual, and, contrary to all his habits, actually offered his hand to assist his bride to rise. Then Diana fell back to the side of the Countess, and Fulk to that of the Earl, and Clarice recognised that the moment of her sacrifice was come.

With one passionately pleading look at the Lady Margaret—who met it as if she had been made of stone—Clarice slowly moved forward to the altar. She shuddered inwardly as Vivian Barkeworth took her hand into his clasp, and answered the queries addressed to her in so low a voice that Father Miles took the words for granted. It seemed only a few minutes before she woke to the miserable truth that she was now Vivian's wife, and that to think any more of Piers Ingham was a sin against God.

Clarice dragged herself through the bridal festivities—how, she never knew. Diana was the life of the party. So bright and gay she was that she might never have heard of such a thing as disappointment. She danced with everybody, entered into all the games with the zest of an eager child, and kept the hall ringing with merry laughter, while Clarice moved through them all as if a weight of lead were upon her, and looked as though she should never smile again. Accident at length threw the two brides close together.

"Art thou going to look thus woe-begone all thy life through, Clarice?" inquired the Lady De Chaucombe.

"I do not know," answered Clarice, gloomily. "I only hope it will not be long."

"What will not be long?—thy sorrowful looks?"

"No—my life."

"Don't let me hear such nonsense," exclaimed Diana, with a little of her old sharpness. "Men are all deceivers, child. There is not one of them worth spoiling a woman's life for. Clarice, don't be a simpleton!"

"Not more than I can help," said Clarice, with the shadow of a smile; and then De Echingham came up and besought her hand for the next dance, and she was caught away again into the whirl.

The dancing, which was so much a matter of course at a wedding, that even the Countess did not venture to interfere with it, was followed by the hoydenish romps which were considered equally necessary, and which fell into final desuetude about the period of the accession of the House of Hanover. King Charles I.'s good taste had led him to frown upon them, and utterly to prohibit them at his own wedding; but the people in general were attached to their amusements, rough and even gross as they often were, and the improvement filtered down from palace to cottage only very slowly.

The cutting of the two bride-cakes, as usual, was one of the most interesting incidents. It was then, and long afterwards, customary to insert three articles in a bride-cake, which were considered to foretel the fortunes of the persons in whose possession they were found when the cakes were cut up. The gold ring denoted speedy marriage; the silver penny indicated future wealth; while the thimble infallibly doomed its recipient to be an old maid. The division of Diana's cake revealed Sir Reginald de Echingham in possession of the ring, evidently to his satisfaction; while Olympias, with the reverse sensation, discovered in her slice both the penny and the thimble. Clarice's cake proved even more productive of mirth; for the thimble fell to the Countess, while the Earl held up the silver penny, laughingly remarking that he was the last person who ought to have had that, since he had already more of them than he wanted. But the fun came to its apex when the ring was discovered in the hand of Mistress Underdone, who indignantly asserted that if a thousand gold rings were showered upon her from as many cakes they would not induce her to marry again. She thought two husbands were enough for any reasonable woman; and if not, she was too old now for folly of that sort. Sir Lambert sent the company into convulsions of laughter by clasping his hands on this announcement with a look of pretended despair, upon which Mistress Underdone, justly indignant, gave him such a box on the ear that he was occupied in rubbing it for the next ten minutes, thereby increasing the merriment of the rest. Loudest and brightest of all the laughers was Diana. She at least had not broken her heart. Clarice, pale and silent in the corner, where she sat and watched the rest, dimly wondered if Diana had any heart to break.

CHAPTER VII.

DAME MAISENTA DOES NOT SEE IT.

"With a little hoard of maxims, preaching down a daughter's heart."
—TENNYSON.

EARL EDMUND had not been callous to the white, woful face under one of the bridal wreaths. He set himself to think how most pleasantly to divert the thoughts of Clarice; and the result of his meditations was a request to Father Miles that he would induce the Countess to invite the parents of Clarice on a visit. The Countess always obeyed Father Miles, though had she known whence the suggestion came, she might have been less docile. A letter, tied up with red silk, and sealed with the Countess's seal, was despatched by a messenger to Dame La Theyn, whom it put into no small flutter of nervous excitement.

A journey to London was a tremendous idea to that worthy woman, though she lived but forty miles from the metropolis. She had never been there in her life. Sir Gilbert had once visited it, and had dilated on the size, splendour, and attractions of the place, till it stood, in the Dame's eyes, next to going to Heaven. It may, indeed, be doubted if she would not have found herself a good deal more at home in the former place than the latter.

Three sumpter-mules were laden with the richest garments and ornaments in the wardrobes of knight and dame. Two armed servants were on one horse, Sir Gilbert and his wife on another ; and thus provided, late in February, they drew bridle at the gate of Whitehall Palace. Clarice had not been told of their coming by the Countess, because she was not sufficiently interested ; by the Earl, because he wished it to be a pleasant surprise. She was called out into the ante-chamber one afternoon, and, to her complete astonishment, found herself in the presence of her parents.

The greeting was tolerably warm.

"Why, child, what hast done to thy cheeks?" demanded Sir Gilbert, when he had kissed his pale-faced daughter. "'Tis all the smoke—that's what it is!"

"Nay ; be sure 'tis the late hours," responded the Dame. "I'll warrant you they go not to bed here afore seven o' the clock. Eh, Clarice?"

"Not before eight, Dame," answered Clarice, with a smile.

"Eight!" cried Dame Maisenta. "Eh, deary me! Mine head to a pod of peas, but that's a hearing! And what time get they up of a morrow?"

"The Lady rises commonly by five or soon after."

"Saint Wulstan be our aid ! Heard I ever the like ? Why, I am never abed after three ! "

"So thou art become Dame Clarice ? " said her father, jovially.

The smile died instantly from Clarice's lips. " Yes," she said, drearily.

"Where is thy knight, lass ? " demanded her mother.

"You will see him in hall," replied Clarice. And when they went down to supper she presented Vivian in due form.

No one knew better than Vivian Barkeworth how to adapt himself to his company. He measured his bride's parents as accurately, in the first five minutes, as a draper would measure a yard of calico. It is not surprising if they were both delighted with him.

The Countess received her guests with careless condescension, the Earl with kind cordiality. Dame La Theyn was deeply interested in seeing both. But her chief aim was a long *tête-à-tête* discourse with Clarice, which she obtained on the day following her arrival. The Countess, as usual, had gone to visit a shrine, and Clarice, being off duty, took her mother to the terrace, where they could chat undisturbed.

Some of us modern folks would rather shrink from sitting on an open terrace in February; but our forefathers were wonderfully independent of the weather, and seem to have been singularly callous in respect to heat and cold. Dame La Theyn made no objection to the airiness of her position, but settled herself comfortably in the corner of the stone bench, and prepared for her chat with much gusto.

"Well, child," was the Dame's first remark, "the good saints have ordered matters rarely for thee. I ventured not to look for such good fortune, not so soon as this. Trust me, but I was rejoiced when I read thy lady's letter, to hear that thou wert well wed unto a knight, and that she had found all the gear. I warrant thee, the grass grew not under my feet afore Dame Rouse, and Mistress Swetapple, and every woman of our neighbours, down to Joan Stick-i'-th'-Lane, knew the good luck that was come to thee."

Clarice sat with her hands in her lap looking out on the river. Good luck! Could Dame La Theyn see no further than that!

"Why, lass, what is come to thee?" demanded the Dame, when she found no response. "Sure, thou art not ungrateful to thy lady for her care and goodness! That were a sin to be shriven for."

Clarice turned her wan face towards her mother.

"Grateful!" she said. "For what should I be thankful to her? Dame, she has torn me away from the only one in the world that I loved, and has forced me to wed a man whom I alike fear and hate. Do you think that matter for thankfulness, or does she!"

"Tut, tut!" said the Dame. "Do not ruffle up thy feathers like a pigeon that has got bread-crumbs when he looked for corn! Why, child, 'tis but what all women have to put up with. We all have our calf-loves and bits of maidenly fancies, but who ever thought they were to rule the roast ?   Sure, Clarice, thou hast more sense than so ? "

"Dame, pardon me, but you understand not. This was no light love of mine—no passing fancy that a newer one might have put out.   It was the one hope and joy of my whole life.   I had nothing else to live for."

To Clarice's horror, the rejoinder to her rhetoric was what the Dame herself would have called "a jolly laugh."

"Dear, dear, how like all young maids be !" cried the mother.   "Just the very thought had I when my good knight my father sent away Master Pride, and told me I must needs wed with thy father, Sir Gilbert.   That is twenty years gone this winter Clarice, and I swear to thee I thought mine heart was broke.   Look on me now.   Look I like a woman that had brake her heart o' love ?   I trow not, by my troth ! "

No; certainly no one would have credited that rosy, comfortable matron with having broken her heart any number of years ago.

"And thou wilt see, too, when twenty years be over, Clarice, I warrant thee thou shalt look back and laugh at thine own folly.   Deary me, child ! Folks cannot weep for ever and the day after. Wait till thou art forty, and then see if thy trouble be as sore in thy mind then as now."

Forty !   Should she ever be forty ?   Clarice fondly hoped not.   And would any lapse of years change the love which seemed to her interwoven with every fibre of her heart? That heart cried out and said, Impossible! But Dame La Theyn heard no answer.

"When thou hast dwelt on middle earth,[1] child, as long as I have, thou wilt look on things more in proportion. There be other affairs in life than love-making. Women spend not all their days thinking of wooing, and men still less. I warrant thee thy lover, whoso he be, shall right soon comfort himself with some other damsel. Never suspect a man of constancy, child. They know not what the word means."

Clarice's inner consciousness violently contradicted this sweeping statement. But she kept silence still.

"Ah, I see!" said her mother, laughing. "Not a word dost thou credit me. I may as well save my breath to cool my porridge. Howsoe'er, Clarice, when thou hast come to forty years, if I am yet alive, let me hear thy thoughts thereupon. Long ere that time come, as sure as eggs be eggs, thou shalt be a-reading the same lesson to a lass of thine, if it please God so to bless thee. And she'll not believe thee a word, any more than thou dost me. Eh, these young folks, these young folks! truly, they be rare fun for us old ones. They think they've gotten all the wisdom that ever dwelt in King Solomon's head, and we may stand aside and doff our caps to them.

---

[1] This mediæval term for the world had its rise in the notion that earth stood midway between Heaven and Hell, the one being as far below as the other was above.

Good lack!—but this world is a queer place, and a merry!"

Clarice thought she had not found it a merry locality by any means.

"And what ails thee at thy knight, child? He is as well-favoured and tall of his hands as e'er a one. Trust me, but I liked him well, and so said thy father. He is a pleasant fellow, no less than a comely. What ails thee at him?"

"Dame, I cannot feel to trust him."

"Give o'er with thy nonsense! Thou mayest trust him as well as another man. They are all alike. They want their own way, and to please themselves, and if they've gotten a bit of time and thought o'er they'll maybe please thee at after. That's the way of the world, child. If thou art one of those silly lasses that look for a man who shall never let his eyes rove from thee, nor never make no love to nobody else, why, thou mayest have thy search for thy pains. Thou art little like to catch that lark afore the sky falls."

Clarice thought that lark had been caught for her, and had been torn from her.

"And what matter?" continued Dame La Theyn. "If a man likes his wife the best, and treats her reasonable kind, as the most do—and I make no doubt thine shall—why should he not have his little pleasures? Thou canst do a bit on thine own account. But mind thou, keep on the windward side o' decency. 'Tis no good committing o' mortal sin,

and a deal o' trouble to get shriven for it. Mind thy
ways afore the world! And let not thy knight get
angered with thee, no more. But I'll tell thee, Clarice,
thou wilt anger him afore long, to carry thyself thus
towards him. Of course a man knows he must put
up with a bit of perversity and bashfulness when he
is first wed; because he can guess reasonable well
that the maid might not have chose him her own
self. But it does not do to keep it up. Thou must
mind thy ways, child."

Clarice was almost holding her breath. Whether
horror or disgust were the feeling uppermost in her
mind, she would have found difficult to tell. Was
this her mother, who gave her such counsel? And
were all women like that? One other distinct idea
was left to her—that there was an additional reason
for dying—to get out of it all.

"Thou art but a simple lass, I can see," reflectively
added Dame La Theyn. "Thou hast right the young
lass's notions touching truth, and faith, and constancy,
and such like. All a parcel of moonshine, child!
There is no such thing, not in this world. Some
folks be a bit worse than others, but that's all. I
dare reckon thy knight is one of the better end. At
any rate, thou wilt find it comfortable to think so."

Clarice was inwardly convinced that Vivian belonged to the scrag end, so far as character went.

"That's the true way to get through the world,
child. Shut thy eyes to whatever thou wouldst not
like to see. Nobody'll admire thee more for having

red rims to 'em. And, dear heart, where's the good? 'Tis none but fools break their hearts. Wise folks jog on jollily. And if there's somewhat to forgive on the one side, why, there'll be somewhat on the other. Thou art not an angel—don't fancy it. And if he isn't neither——"

Of that fact Clarice felt superlatively convinced.

"The best way is not to expect it of him, and thou wilt be the less disappointed. So get out thy ribbons and busk thee, and let's have no more tears shed. There's been a quart too much already."

A slight movement of nervous impatience was the sole reply.

"Eh, Clarice? Ne'er a word, trow?"

Then she turned round a wan, set, distressed face, with fervent determination glowing in the eyes.

"Mother! I would rather die, and be out of it!"

"Be out of what, quotha?" demanded Dame La Theyn, in astonished tones.

"This world," said Clarice, through her set teeth. "This hard, cold, cruel, miserable, wicked world. Is there only one of two lives before me—either to harden into stone and crush other hearts, or to be crushed by the others that have got hard before me? Oh, Mother, Mother! is there nothing in the world for a woman but *that?*—God, let me die before I come to either!"

"Deary, deary, deary me!" seemed to be all that Dame La Theyn felt herself capable of saying.

"A few weeks ago," Clarice went on, "before—

this, there was a higher and better view of life given to me. One that would make one's crushed heart grow softer, and not harder; that was upward and not downward; that led to Heaven and God, not to Hell and Satan. There is no hope for me in this life but the hope of Heaven. For pity's sake let me keep that! If every other human creature is going down—you seem to think so—let me go higher, not lower. Because my life has been spoiled for me, shall I deliberately poison my own soul? May God forbid it me! If I am to spend my life with demons, let my spirit live with God."

The feelings of Dame La Theyn, on hearing this speech from Clarice, were not capable of expression in words.

In her eyes, as in those of all Romanists, there were two lives which a man or woman could lead— the religious and the secular. To lead a religious life meant, as a matter of course, to go into the cloister. Matrimony and piety were simply incompatible. Clarice was a married woman: *ergo*, she could not possibly be religious. Dame La Theyn's mind, to use one of her favourite expressions, was all of a jumble with these extraordinary ideas of which her daughter had unaccountably got hold. "What on earth is the child driving at? is she mad?" thought her mother.

"What dost thou mean, child?" inquired the extremely puzzled Dame. "Thou canst not go into the cloister—thou art wed. Dear heart, but I never reckoned thou hadst any vocation! Thou shouldst have told thy lady."

"I do not want the cloister," said Clarice. "I want to do God's will. I want to belong to God."

"Why, that is the same thing!" responded the still perplexed woman.

"The Lord Earl is not a monk," replied Clarice. "And I am sure he belongs to God, for he knows Him better than any priest that I ever saw."

"Child, child! Did I not tell thee, afore ever thou camest into this house, that thy Lord was a man full of queer fancies, and all manner of strange things? Don't thee go and get notions into thine head, for mercy's sake! Thou must live either in the world or the cloister. Who ever heard of a wedded woman devote to religion? Thou canst not have both—'tis nonsense. Is that one of thy Lord's queer notions? Sure, these friars never taught thee so?"

"The friars never taught me anything. Father Bevis tried to help me, but he did not know how. My Lord was the only one who understood."

"Understood? Understood what?"

"Who understood me, and who understood God."

"Clarice, what manner of tongue art thou talking? 'Tis none I never learned."

No, for Clarice was beginning to lisp the language of Canaan, and "they that kept the fair were men of this world." What wonder if she and her thoroughly time-serving mother found it impossible to understand each other?

"I cannot make thee out, lass. If thou wert aware afore thou wert wed that thou hadst a vocation, 'twas right wicked of thee not to tell thy confessor and thy mistress, both. But I cannot see how it well could, when thou wert all head o'er ears o' love with some gallant or other—the saints know whom. I reckon it undecent, in very deed, Clarice, to meddle up a love-tale with matters of religion. I do wonder thou hast no more sense of fitness and decorum."

"It were a sad thing," said Clarice quietly, "if only irreligious people might love each other."

"Love each other! Dear heart, thy brains must be made o' forcemeat! Thou hast got love, and religion, and living, and all manner o' things, jumbled up together in a pie. They've nought to do with each other, thou silly lass."

"If religion has nought to do with living, Dame, under your good pleasure, what has it to do with?"

A query which Dame La Theyn found it as difficult to comprehend as to answer. In her eyes, religion was a thing to take to church on Sunday, and life was restricted to the periods when people were not in church. When she laid up her Sunday gown in lavender, she put her religion in with it. Of course, nuns were religious every day, but nobody else ever thought of such an unreasonable thing. Clarice's new ideas, therefore, to her, were simply preposterous and irrational.

"Clarice!" she said, in tones of considerable

surprise, "I do wonder what's come o'er thee!
This is not the lass I sent to Oakham. Have the
fairies been and changed thee, or what on earth has
happened to thee ? I cannot make thee out ! "

"I hardly know what has happened to me," was
the answer, "but I think it is that I have gone
nearer God. He ploughed up my heart with the
furrow of bitter sorrow, and then He made it soft
with the dew of His grace. I suppose the seed
will come next. What that is I do not know yet.
But my knowing does not matter if He knows."

The difference which Dame La Theyn failed to
understand was the difference between life and
death. The words of the Earl had been used as
a seed of life, and the life was growing. It is the
necessity of life to grow, and it is an impossibility
that death should appreciate life.

"Well!" was the Dame's conclusion, delivered as
she rose from the stone bench, in a perplexed and
disappointed tone, "I reckon thou wilt be like to
take thine own way, child, for I cannot make either
head or tail of thy notions. Only I do hope thou
wilt not set up to be unlike everybody else. Depend
upon it, Clarice, a woman never comes to no good
when she sets up to be better than her neighbours.
It is bad enough in anybody, but 'tis worser in a
woman than a man. I cannot tell who has stuck thy
queer notions into thee—whether 'tis thy Lord, or
thy lover, or who; but I would to all the saints he
had let thee be. I liked thee a deal better afore, I

can tell thee. I never had no fancy for philosophy and such."

"Mother," said Clarice softly, "I think it was God."

"Gently, child! No bad language, prithee." Dame La Theyn looked upon pious language as profanity when uttered in an unconsecrated place. "But if it were the Almighty that put these notions into thy head, I pray He'll take 'em out again."

"I think not," quietly replied Clarice.

And so the scene closed, Neither had understood the other, so far, at least, as spiritual matters were concerned. But in respect to the secular question Dame La Theyn could enter into Clarice's thoughts more than she chose to allow. The dialogue stirred within her faint memories—not quite dead—of that earlier time when her tears had flowed for the like cause, and when she had felt absolutely certain that she could never be happy again. But her love had been of a selfish and surface kind, and the wound, never more than skin-deep, had healed rapidly and left no scar. Was it surprising if she took it for granted that her daughter's was of the same class, and would heal with equal rapidity and completeness? Beside this, she thought it very unwise policy to let Clarice perceive that she did understand her in any wise. It would encourage her in her folly, Dame La Theyn considered, if she supposed that so wise a person as her mother could have any sympathy with such notions. So she wrapped herself complacently in her mantle of wisdom, and never perceived that she was severing the last strand of the rope which bound her child's heart to her own.

"O, purblind race of miserable men !"

How strangely we all spend our lives in the anxious labour of straining out gnats, while we scarcely detect the moment when we swallow the camel!

A long private conversation between Clarice's parents resulted the next day in Sir Gilbert taking her in hand. His comprehension was even less than her mother's, though it lay in a different direction.

"Well, Clarice, my dame tells me thou art not altogether well pleased with thy wedding. What didst thou wish otherwise, lass ?"

"The man," said Clarice, shortly enough.

"What, is not one man as good as another?" demanded her father.

"Not to me, Sir," said his daughter.

"I am afeared, Clarice, thou hast some romantic notions. They are all very pretty to play with, but they don't do for this world, child. Thou hast better shake them out of thine head, and be content with thy lot."

"It is a bad world, I know," replied Clarice. "But it is hard to be content, when life has been emptied and spoiled for one."

"Folly, child, folly !" said Sir Gilbert. "Thou mayest have as many silk gowns now as thou couldst have had with any other knight; and I dare be bound Sir Vivian should give thee a gold chain if thou wert pining for it. Should that content thee?"

"No, Sir."

Sir Gilbert was puzzled. A woman whose perfect happiness could not be secured by a gold chain was an enigma to him.

"Then what would content thee?" he asked.

"What I can never have now," answered Clarice. "It may be, as time goes on, that God will make me content without it—content with His will, and no more. But I doubt if even He could do that just yet. The wisest physician living cannot heal a wound in a minute. It must have its time."

Sir Gilbert tried to puzzle his way through this speech.

"Well, child, I do not see what I can do for thee."

"I thank you for wishing it, fair Sir. No, you can do nothing. No one can do anything for me, except let me alone, and pray to God to heal the wound."

"Well, lass, I can do that," said her father, brightening. "I will say the rosary all over for thee once in the week, and give a candle to our Lady. Will that do thee a bit of good, eh?"

Clarice had an instinctive feeling, that while the rosary and the candle might be a doubtful good, the rough tenderness of her father was a positive one. Little as Sir Gilbert could enter into her ideas, his affection was truer and more unselfish than that of her mother. Neither of them was very deeply attached to her; but Sir Gilbert's love could have borne the harder strain of the two. Clarice began to recognise the fact with touched surprise.

"Fair Sir, I shall be very thankful for your prayers. It will do me good to be loved—so far as anything can do it."

Sir Gilbert was also discovering, with a little astonishment himself, that his only child lay nearer to his heart than he had supposed. His heart was a plant which had never received much cultivation, either from himself or any other; and love, even in faint throbs, was a rather strange sensation. It made him feel as if something were the matter with him, and he could not exactly tell what. He patted Clarice's shoulder, and smoothed down her hair.

"Well, well, child! I hope all things will settle comfortably by and by. But if they should not, and in especial if thy knight were ever unkindly toward thee—which God avert!—do not forget that thou hast a friend in thine old father. Maybe he has not shown thee over much kindliness neither, but I reckon, my lass, if it came to a pull, there'd be a bit to pull at."

Neither Sir Gilbert nor Dame Maisenta ever fully realised the result of that visit. It found Clarice indifferent to both, but ready to reach out a hand to either who would clasp it with any appearance of tenderness and compassion. It left her with a heart closed for ever to her mother, but for ever open to her father.

CHAPTER VIII.

THE SHADOW OF THE FUTURE.

In His name was struck the blow
That hath laid thy old life low
In a garb of blood-red woe.

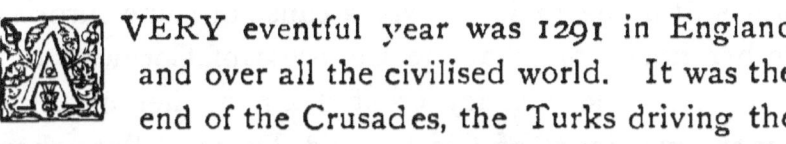 VERY eventful year was 1291 in England and over all the civilised world. It was the end of the Crusades, the Turks driving the Christians from Acre, the last place which they held in Palestine. It opened with the submission of the Scottish succession to the arbitrament of Edward the First, and it closed with the funeral of his mother, Queen Eléonore of Provence—a woman whom England was not able to thank for one good deed during her long and stormy reign. She had been a youthful beauty, she wrote poetry, and she had never scandalised the nation by any impropriety of womanly conduct. But these three statements close the list of her virtues. She was equally grasping, unscrupulous, and extravagant. In her old age she retired to the Convent of Amesbury, where her two granddaughters, Mary of England, and Alianore of

Bretagne, were nuns already, for the desirable purpose of "making her salvation." Perhaps she thought she had made it when the summons came to her in the autumn of 1291. No voice had whispered to her, all through her long life of nearly eighty years, that if that ever were to be—

> "Jesus Christ has done it all
> Long, long ago."

Matters had settled down quietly enough in White-hall Palace. Sir Fulk de Chaucombe and Diana had been promoted to the royal household—the former as attendant upon the King, the latter as Lady of the Bedchamber to his eldest daughter, the Princess Alianora, who, though twenty-seven years of age, was still unmarried. It was a cause of some surprise in her household that the Countess of Cornwall did not fill up the vacancy created among her maidens by the marriages of Clarice and Diana. But when December came it was evident that before she did so she meant to make the vacancy still more complete.

One dark afternoon in that cheerful month, the Lady Margaret marched into the bower, where her female attendants usually sat when not engaged in more active waiting upon her. It was Saturday.

"Olympias Trusbut, Roisia de Levinton," she said in her harsh voice, which did not sound unlike the rasping of a file, "ye are to be wed on Monday morning."

Olympias showed slight signs of going into hysterics, which being observed by the Lady Margaret, she calmly desired Felicia to fetch a jug of water. On this hint of what was likely to happen to her if she imprudently screamed or fainted, Olympias managed to recover.

"Ye are to wed the two squires," observed their imperious mistress. " I gave the choice to Reginald de Echingham, and he fixed on thee, Olympias."

Olympias passed from terror to ecstasy.

"Thou, Roisia, art to wed Ademar de Gernet. I will give both of you your gear."

And away walked the Countess.

" I wish she would have let me alone," said Roisia, in doleful accents.

" Too much to hope for," responded Felicia.

"Dost thou not like De Gernet?" asked Clarice, sympathisingly.

" Oh, I don't dislike him," said Roisia; " but I am not so fond of him as that comes to."

An hour or two later, however, Mistress Under-done appeared, in a state of flurry by no means her normal one.

" Well, here is a pretty tale," said she. " Not for thee, Olympias; matters be running smooth for thee, though the Lord Earl did say," added she, laughing, " that incense was as breath of life to Narcissus, and he would needs choose the maid that should burn plenty on his altar. But—the thing is fair unheard of!—Ademar de Gernet refuses to wed under direc-tion from the Lady."

" Why?" asked Roisia, looking rather insulted.

"Oh, it has nought to do with thee, child," said Mistress Underdone. "Quoth he that he desired all happiness to thee, and pardon of thee for thus dealing; but having given his heart to another of the Lady's damsels, he would not wed with any but her."

"Why, that must be Felicia," said the other three together.

Felicia looked flattered and conscious.

"Well, I reckon so," answered Mistress Underdone. "Howbeit, the Lady hath sent for him hither, to know of him in thy presence what he would be at."

"*Ha, chétife!*" exclaimed Roisia. "I wish it had been somewhere else."

"Well, I cannot quite——. Hush! here she comes."

And for the second time that day in stalked the Countess, and sat down on the curule chair which Mistress Underdone set for her, looking like a judge, and a very stern one, too. In another minute the culprit made his appearance, in charge of Sir Lambert Aylmer.

"Now, De Gernet, what means this?" irascibly demanded his mistress.

"Lady, it means not disobedience to you, nor any displeasance done to this young damsel"—and De Gernet turned and bowed to Roisia. "This it means, that I dearly love another of your Ladyship's damsels, and I do most humbly and heartily crave your permission to wed with her."

"What, Felicia de Fay?" said the Countess.

"Under your Ladyship's pleasure and her pardon, no."

Felicia's face changed evilly.

"But who, then? There is none other."

"Let my Lady be pleased to pardon me. There is one other—Heliet Pride."

The faces in the bower just then might have furnished a study for an artist. Those of Clarice and Olympias expressed surprise mixed with some pleasure; so did Mistress Underdone's, but the degree of both was intense. The Countess looked half vexed and wholly astonished, with a little contempt superadded. Felicia's face foreboded nothing but ill to either Ademar or Heliet.

"Heliet Pride!" cried the Countess sharply. "Why, man, she goes on crutches!"

"They will carry her to the chapel, with my Lady's leave," answered De Gernet, coolly.

"Gramercy, but thou wilt have a lovely wife! There'll be no pride in her outside her name," said the Countess, with a grim smile at her own joke. Indeed, she was so much amused that she forgot to be angry.

"I will see about that, if my Lady will grant me her grace," responded De Gernet, in the same tone.

"Eh, thou shalt have her," said the Countess. "I shall get Roisia disposed of a sight easier than Heliet. So be it. Roisia, thou canst still prepare for thy bridal; I will find somebody by Monday morning."

The Countess was rising from her chair, when Sir Lambert, after a glance at Roisia, observed that if her Ladyship found any difficulty in that selection, he had no particular objection to be chosen.

"You!" said the Countess. "Oh, very good; it will save trouble. Let it be so."

Roisia appeared to be, if anything, rather gratified by the exchange. But Clarice, looking into the dark, passionate eyes of Felicia, felt troubled for the happiness of Heliet.

Olympias, like Clarice, was promoted to a vacancy among the ladies of the bedchamber. But Sir Lambert and Roisia passed away from the life at Whitehall. The new Maids of Honour were speedily appointed. Their names proved to be Sabina Babingell, Ada Gresley, and Filomena Bray. The Countess declared her intention of keeping four only in the future.

The summer of 1292 saw the King on the Scottish border, and in his train the Earl and Countess of Cornwall, with their household, moved north as far as Oakham. The household had been increased by one more, for in the April previous Clarice Barkeworth became the mother of a little girl.

This was the first event which helped to reconcile her to her lot. She had been honestly trying hard to do her duty by Vivian, who scarcely seemed to think that he had any duty towards her, beyond the obvious one of civility in public. All thought of Piers Ingham had been resolutely crushed down, except when it came—as it sometimes did—in the form of a dream of bliss from which she awoke to desolation. A miserable day was sure to follow one of those dreams. The only other moment when she allowed herself to think of him was in her evening prayer.

It was a relief to Clarice that she had never heard a word of Piers since he left Whitehall. Her work would have been harder if his name had remained a household word. And yet in another sense it was hard never to know what had become of him, whether he were as sad as herself, or had been comforted elsewhere.

Vivian's manners in public were perfect to every one, and Clarice shared with the rest. In private she was terribly snubbed whenever he was in a bad temper, and carelessly ignored when he was in a good one. The baby daughter, who was such a comfort to Clarice, was a source of bitter vexation to Vivian. In his eyes, while a son would have been an undoubted blessing, a daughter was something actively worse than a disappointment. When Clarice timidly inquired what name he wished the child to bear, Vivian distinctly intimated that the child and all her belongings were totally beneath his notice. She could call the nuisance what she liked.

Clarice silently folded her insulted darling to her breast, and tacitly promised it that its mother at least should never think it a nuisance.

"What shall I call her?" she said to Mistress

Underdone and Olympias, both of whom were inclined to pet the baby exceedingly.

"Oh, something pretty!" said Olympias. "Don't
have a plain, common name. Don't call her Joan,
or Parnel, or Beatrice, or Margery, or Maud, or
Isabel. You meet those at every turn. I am quite
glad I was not called anything of that sort."

"I wouldn't have it too long," was Mistress Underdone's recommendation. "I'd never call her Frethe-
sancia, or Florianora, or Aniflesia, or Sauncelina.
Let her have a good, honest name, Dame, one
syllable, or at most two. You'll have to clip it
otherwise."

"I thought of Rose," said Clarice, meditatively.

"Well, it is not common," allowed Olympias.
"Still, it is very short. Couldn't you have had it a
little longer?"

"That'll do," pronounced Mistress Underdone. "It
is short, and it means a pretty, sweet, pleasant thing.
I don't know but I should have called my girl Rose,
if I'd chosen her name; but her father fancied Heliet,
and so it had to be so."

"Well, we can call her Rosamond," comfortingly
suggested Olympias.

So, in the course of that evening, Father Bevis
baptized little Rose Barkeworth in the chapel of the
palace, the Earl standing sponsor for her, with the
Lady de Chaucombe and the Lady de Echingham.
The Countess had been asked, but to Clarice's private
satisfaction had declined, for she would much rather

have had the Earl, and the canon law forbade husband and wife being sponsors to the same infant.

Something was the matter with the Countess. Every one agreed upon this, but nobody could guess what it was. She was quieter than her wont, and was given to long, silent reveries, which had not been usual with her.

Filomena, who was of a lively turn of mind, declared that life at Whitehall was becoming absolutely intolerable, and that she should be thankful to go to Oakham, for at least it would be something new.

"Thou wilt be thankful to come away again," said Mistress Underdone, with a smile.

They reached Oakham about the middle of July, and found Heliet, leaning on her crutches, ready to welcome them with smiles in the hall. No news had reached her of their proceedings, and there was a great deal to tell her; but Heliet and the baby took to one another in an instant, as if by some unseen magical force.

The item of news which most concerned herself was not told to Heliet that night. The next morning, when all were seated at work, and baby Rose, in Heliet's lap, was contentedly sucking her very small thumb, Mistress Underdone said rather suddenly, "We have not told thee all, Heliet."

"I dare say not," replied Heliet, brightly. "You must have all done a great deal more in these two years than you have told me."

"Well, lass, 'tis somewhat I never looked I should have to tell thee. There's somebody wants to wed thee."

"ME!" cried Heliet, in large capitals.

"Ay, thee—crutches and all," said her mother laughing. "He said he did not care for thy crutches so they carried thee safe to chapel; and he ran the risk of offending the Lady to get thee. So I reckon he sets some store by thee, lass."

"Who is it?" said Heliet, in a low voice, while a bright red spot burned in each cheek.

"Ademar de Gernet." Two or three voices told her. The bright spots burned deeper.

"Is it to be?" was the next question.

"Ay, the Lady said so much; and I reckon she shall give thee thy gear."

"God has been very good to me," said Heliet, softly, rocking little Rose gently to and fro. "But I never thought He meant to give me *that*."

Clarice looked up, and saw a depth of happy love in the lame girl's eyes, which made her sigh for herself. Then, looking further, she perceived a depth of black hate in those of Felicia de Fay, which made her tremble for Heliet.

It appeared very shortly that the Countess was in a hurry to get the wedding over. Perhaps she was weary of weddings in her household, for she did not seem to be in a good temper about this. She always thought Heliet would have had a vocation, she said, which would have been far better for her, with her lameness, than to go limping into chapel to be wed. She wondered nobody saw the impropriety of it. However, as she had promised De Gernet, she supposed it must be so. She did not know what she herself could have been thinking about to make such a foolish promise. She was not usually so silly as that. However, if it must be, it had better be got over.

So got over it was, on an early morning in August, De Gernet receiving knighthood from the Earl at the close of the ceremony.

Mistress Underdone had petitioned that her lame and only child might not be separated from her, and the Countess—according to her own authority, in a moment of foolishness—had granted the petition. So Heliet was drafted among the Ladies of the Bed-chamber, but only as an honorary distinction.

The manner of the Countess continued to strike every one as unusual. Long fits of musing with hands lying idle were becoming common with her, and when she rose from them she would generally shut herself up in her oratory for the remainder of the day. Clarice thought, and Heliet agreed with her, that something was going to happen. Once, too, as Clarice was carrying Rose along the terrace, she was met by the Earl, who stopped and noticed the child, as in his intense and unsatisfied love for little children he always did. Clarice thought he looked even unwontedly sorrowful.

From the child, Earl Edmund looked up into the pleased eyes of the young mother.

"Dame Clarice," he asked, gently, "are you happier than you were?"

Her eyes grew suddenly grave.

"Thus far," she said, touching the child. "Otherwise—I try to be content with God's will, fair Lord. It is hard to bear heart-hunger."

"Ah!" The Earl's tone was significant. "Yes, it is hard to bear in any form," he said, after a pause. "May God send you never to know, Dame, that there is a more terrible form than that wherein you bear it."

And he left her almost abruptly.

The winter of 1292 dragged slowly along. Filomena declared that her body was as starved as her mind, and she should be frozen to death if she stayed any longer. The next day, to everybody's astonishment, the Countess issued orders to pack up for travelling. Sir Vivian and Clarice were to go with her—where, she did not say. So were Olympias, Felicia, and Ada. Mistress Underdone, Sir Reginald, Sir Ademar and Heliet, Filomena and Sabina, were left behind at Oakham.

Olympias grumbled extremely at being separated from her husband, and Filomena at being left behind. The Countess would listen to neither.

"When shall we return, under my Lady's leave?" asked Olympias, disconsolately.

"*You* can return," was the curt answer, "when I have done with you. I doubt if Sir Vivian and his dame will return at all. Ada certainly will not."

" *Ha. jolife !* " said Ada, under her breath. She did not like Oakham.

Clarice, on the contrary, was inclined to make an exclamation of horror. For never to return to Oakham meant never to see Heliet again. And what could the Countess mean by a statement which sounded at least as if *she* were not intending to return ?

Concerning Felicia the Countess said nothing. That misnamed young lady had during the past few months been trying her best to make Heliet miserable. She began by attempting to flirt with Sir Ademar, but she found him completely impervious material. Her arrows glanced upon his shield, and simply dropped off without further notice. Then she took to taunting Heliet with her lameness, but Heliet kept her temper. Next she sneered at her religious views. Heliet answered her gently, gravely, but held her own with undiminished calmness. This point had been reached when the Countess's order was given to depart from Oakham.

Even those least disposed to note the signs of the times felt the pressure of some impending calamity. The strange manner of the Countess, the restless misery of the Earl, whom they all loved, the busy, bustling, secretly-triumphant air of Father Miles— all denoted some hidden working. Father Bevis had been absent for some weeks, and when he returned he wore the appearance of a baffled and out-wearied man.

"He looks both tired and disappointed," remarked Clarice to Heliet.

"He looks," said Heliet, "like a man who had been trying very hard to scale the wall of a tower, and had been flung back, bruised and helpless, upon the stones below."

During the four months last spent at Oakham, Clarice had been absolutely silent to Heliet on the subject of her own peculiar trouble. Perhaps she might have remained so, had it not been for the approaching separation. But her lips were unsealed by the strong possibility that they might never meet again. It was late on the last evening that Clarice spoke, as she sat rocking Rose's cradle. She laid bare her heart before Heliet's sympathising eyes, until she could trace the whole weary journey through the arid desert sands.

"And now tell me, friend," Clarice ended, "why our Lord deals so differently with thee and with me. Are we not both His children? Yet to thee He hath given the desire of thine heart, and on mine He lays His hand, and says, 'No, child, thou must not have it.'"

"I suppose, beloved," was Heliet's gentle answer, "that the treatment suitable for consumption will not answer for fever. We are both sick of the deadly disease of sin; but it takes a different development in each. Shall we wonder if the Physician bleeds the one, and administers strengthening medicines to the other?"

Clarice's lip quivered, but she rocked Rose's cradle without answering.

"There is also another consideration," pursued Heliet. "If I mistake not—to alter the figure—we have arrived at different points in our education. If one of us can but decline '*puer*,' while the other is half through the syntax, is it any wonder if the same lesson be not given to us to learn? Dear Clarice, all God's children need keeping down. I have been kept down all these years by my physical sufferings. That is not appointed to thee; thou art tried in another way. Shall we either marvel or murmur because our Father sees that each needs a different class of discipline?"

"Oh, Heliet, if I might have had thine! It seems to me so much the lighter cross to carry."

"Then, dear, I am the less honoured—the further from the full share of the fellowship of our Lord's sufferings."

Clarice shook her head as if she hardly saw it in that light.

"Clarice, let me tell thee a parable which I read the other day in the writings of the holy Fathers. There were once two monks, dwelling in hermits' cells near to each other, each of whom had one choice tree given him to cultivate. When this had lasted a year, the tree of the one was in flourishing health, while that of the other was all stunted and bare. 'Why, brother,' said the first, 'what hast thou done to thy tree?' 'Now, judge thou, my brother,' replied the second, 'if I could possibly have done

K

more for my tree than I have done. I watched it carefully every day. When I thought it looked dry, I prayed for rain; when the ground was too wet, I prayed for dry weather; I prayed for north wind or south wind, as I saw them needed. All that I asked, I received; and yet look at my poor tree! But how didst thou treat thine? for thy plan has been so much more successful than mine that I would fain try it next year.' The other monk said only, 'I prayed God to make my tree flourish, and left it to Him to send what weather He saw good.'"

"He has sent a bitter blast from the north-east," answered Clarice, with trembling lips.

"And a hedge to shelter the root of the tree," said Heliet, pointing to Rose.

"Oh, my little Rosie!" exclaimed Clarice, kissing the child passionately. "But if God were to take her, Heliet, what would become of me?"

"Do not meet trouble half way, dear," said Heliet, gently. "There is no apparent likelihood of any such thing."

"I do not meet it—it comes!" cried poor Clarice.

"Then wait till it comes. 'Sufficient unto the day is the evil thereof.'"

"Yet when one has learned by experience that evil is perpetually coming, how can one help looking forward to the morrow?"

"Look forward," said Heliet. "But let it be to the day after to-morrow — the day when we shall awake up after Christ's likeness, and be satisfied with it—when the Lord our God shall come, and all the saints with Him. Dear, a gem cannot be engraved without the cutting-tools. Wouldst thou rather be spared the pain of the cutting than have Christ's likeness graven upon thee ?"

" Oh, could it not be done with less cutting ?"

" Yes—and more faintly graven then."

Clarice sobbed, without speaking.

" If the likeness is to be in high relief, so that all men may see it, and recognise the resemblance, and applaud the graver, Clarice, the tool must cut deep."

" If one could ever know that it was nearly done, it would be easier to bear it."

" Ay, but how if the vision were granted us, and we saw that it was not nearly done by many a year ? It is better not to know, dear. Yet it is natural to us all to think that it would be far easier if we could see. Therefore the more 'blessed is he that hath not seen, and yet hath believed.'"

" I do think," said poor Clarice, drearily, "that I must be the worst tried of all His people."

" Clarice," answered Heliet, in a low voice, " I believe there is one in this very castle far worse tried than thou—a cross borne which is ten times heavier than thine, and has no rose-bud twined around it. And it is carried with the patience of an angel, with the unselfish forgetfulness of Christ. The tool is going very deep there, and already the portrait stands out in beautiful relief. And that cross will never be laid down till the sufferer parts with it

at the very gate of Heaven.   At least, so it seems to
me.   As the years go on it grows heavier, and it is
crushing him almost into the dust now."

"Whom dost thou mean, Heliet?"

"The Lord Earl, our master."

"I can see he is sorely tried; but I never quite
understand what his trouble is."

"The sorrow of being actively hated by the only
one whom he loves.   The prospect of being left to
die, in wifeless and childless loneliness—that terrible
loneliness of soul which is so much worse to bear
than any mere physical solitude.   God, for some
wise reason, has shut him up to Himself.   He has
deprived him of all human relationship and human
love; has said to him, 'Lean on Me, and walk loose
from all other ties.'   A wedded man in the eyes of
the world, God has called him in reality to be an
anchorite of the Order of Providence, to follow the
Lamb whithersoever He goeth.   And unless mine
eyes see very wrongly into the future—as would God
they did!—the Master is about to lead this dear
servant into the Gethsemane of His passion, that he
may be fashioned like Him in all things.   Ah,
Clarice, that takes close cutting!"

"Heliet, what dost thou mean?   Canst thou guess
what the Lady is about to do?"

"I think she is going to leave him."

"Alone?—for ever?"

"For earth," said Heliet, softly.   "God be thanked,
that is **not** for ever."

"What an intensely cruel woman she is!" cried Clarice, indignantly.

"Because, I believe, she is a most miserable one."

"Canst thou feel any pity for *her?*"

"It is not so easy as for him. Yet I suspect she needs it even more than he does. Christ have mercy on them both!"

"I cannot comprehend it," said Clarice.

"I will tell thee one thing," answered Heliet. "I would rather change with thee than with Sir Edmund the Earl; and a hundred times rather with thee than with the Lady Margaret. It is hard to suffer; but it is worse to be the occasion of suffering. Let me die a thousand times over with St. Stephen, before I keep the clothes of the persecutors with Saul."

Clarice stooped and lifted the child from the cradle.

"It is growing late," she said. "I suppose we ought not to be up longer. Good-night, sweetheart, and many thanks for thy counsel. It is all true, I know; yet——"

"In twenty years, may be — or at the longest, when thou hast seen His Face in righteousness— dear Clarice, thou wilt know it, and want to add no *yet.*"

The soft tap of Heliet's crutches had died away, but Clarice stood still with the child in her arms.

"It must be *yet* now, however," she said, half aloud. "Do Thy will with me—cut me and perfect me; but, O God, leave me, leave me Rosie!"

CHAPTER IX.

OVERWHELMED.

"I am a useless and an evil man,—
God planned my life, and let men spoil His plan."
—Isabella Fyvie Mayo.

AKHAM was left behind; and to the surprise of the party—except the Countess, her Prime Minister, Father Miles, and her Foreign Secretary, Felicia—they found themselves lodged in Rochester Castle. Here the Countess shut herself up, and communicated with the outward world through her Cabinet only. All orders were brought to the ladies by Felicia, and were passed to Vivian by Father Miles. The latter was closeted with his lady for long periods, and rolls of writing appeared to be the result of these conferences.

The winter moved on with leaden feet, according to the ideas of the household, and of Ada more particularly.

"This sort of life is really something dreadful!" said that young lady. "If the frost would only break up, it would make something fresh to look at. There is *nothing* to be done!"

"Poor Ada!" responded Olympias, laughing. "Do get some needlework."

"I am tired of needlework," answered Ada. "I am tired of everything!"

Felicia came in as the words were spoken.

"I have permission to tell you something," she said, with a light in her black eyes which Clarice felt sure meant mischief. "The Lady has appealed to the holy Father for a divorce from the Lord Earl."

"Will she get it?" asked Olympias.

"No doubt of it," replied Felicia dogmatically.

"And if so, what will she do then?" asked Ada.

"Her pious intention," said Felicia, the black eyes dancing, "is to become a holy Sister of the Order of the blessed Saint Dominic."

"Then what is to become of the Lord Earl?" queried Olympias. "I suppose he can marry somebody else. I hope he will."

"That is no concern of the Lady's," said Felicia, in a tone of pious severity. "The religious do not trouble their holy repose about externs, except to offer prayers for their salvation."

"Why, then, we shall all be turned out!" blankly cried Ada. "What is to become of us all?"

"What will become of me is already settled," replied Felicia demurely. "I am about to make profession in the same convent with my mistress."

"Thank the saints!" reached Clarice's ears in a

whisper from Olympias, and was deliberately echoed in the heart of the former.

"But that will never do for me!" exclaimed Ada. "I am sure I have no vocation. What am I to do?"

"The Lady proposes, in her goodness," said the Countess's mouthpiece, "to get thee an appointment in the household of one of the Ladies the King's daughters."

"*Ha, jolife!*" said Ada, and ceased her interjections.

"For you, Dames," continued Felicia, turning to Clarice and Olympias, "she says that, being wedded, you are already provided for, and need no thought on her part."

"Oh, then, I may go back to Oakham," answered Olympias in a satisfied tone. "That is what I want."

Clarice wondered sorrowfully what her lot would be—whether she might return to Oakham. She felt more at home there than anywhere else. The question was whether, Clarice being now at large, Vivian would continue in the Earl's service; and even if he did, they might perhaps no longer live in the Castle. Clarice took this new trouble where she carried them all; but the Earl's sorrow was more in her mind than her own. She was learning to cultivate

> "A heart at leisure from itself,
>   To soothe and sympathise."

She found that Vivian had already heard the news from Father Miles, and she timidly ventured to ask him what he intended to do.

After a few flights of rhetoric concerning the extreme folly of the Countess—to forsake an earldom for the cloister was a proceeding not in Vivian's line at all—that gentleman condescended so far to answer his wife as to observe that he was not fool enough not to know when he was well off. Clarice thankfully conjectured that they would return to Oakham. She thought it better, however, to ask the question point blank; and she received a reply —of course accompanied by a snub.

"Why should we be such fools as to go to Oakham when my Lord is in Bermondsey?"

"Bermondsey!" Clarice was surprised.

"You never know anything!" said Vivian. "Of course he is come to town."

Clarice received the snubbing in silence.

"You are so taken up with that everlasting brat of yours," added Rose's affectionate father, "that you never know what anybody else is doing."

There had been a time when Clarice would have defended herself against such accusations. She was learning now that she suffered least when she received them in meek silence. The only way to deal with Vivian Barkeworth was to let him alone.

Two long letters went to the Pope that February; one was from the Countess, the other from the Earl. They are both yet extant, and they show the character of each as no description could set it forth.

The Countess's letter is a mixture of pious demureness and querulous selfishness. She tells the Pope

that all her life she has intensely desired to be a
nun: that she is, unhappily, in the irreligious
position of a matron, and, moreover, is the suffering wife of an impious husband. This sinful man
requires of her—of her, a soul devoted to religion—
that she shall behave as if she belonged to the
wicked world which holds himself within its thrall,
and shall sacrifice God to him. She humbly and
fervently entreats the holy Father to grant her a
divorce from these bonds of matrimony which so
cruelly oppress her, and to set her soul free that it
may soar upwards unrestrained. It is the letter of
a woman who did wish to serve God, but who was
incapable of recognising that it was possible to do
it without shutting herself up in stone walls, and
starving body and soul alike.

The Earl's letter is of an entirely different calibre.
He tells the Pope in his turn that he is wedded to
a woman whom he dearly loves, and who resolutely
keeps him at arm's length. She will not make a
friend of him, nor behave as a good wife ought to
do. This is all he asks of her; he is as far as can
be from wishing to be unkind to her or to cross her
wishes. He only wants her to live with him on
reasonable and ordinary terms. But she—and here
the Earl's irrepressible humour breaks out; he must
see the comical side even of his own sorest trouble,
and certainly this had its comical side—she will not
sit next to him at table, but insists on putting her
confessor between; she will not answer Yes or No

to his simplest question, but invariably returns the answer through a third person. When she goes into her private apartments, she turns the key in his face. Does the holy Father think this is the way that a rational wife ought to behave to her own husband? and will he not remonstrate with her, and induce her to use him a little more kindly and reasonably than she does? The Earl's letter is that of an injured and justly provoked man; of a man who loves his wife too well to coerce or quarrel with her, and who thoroughly perceives the absurdity of his position no less than its pain. Yet he does feel the pain bitterly, and he would do anything to end it.

This letter to the Patriarch of Christendom was his last hope. Entreaties, remonstrances, patient tenderness, loving kindness, all had proved vain. Now

> "He had set his life upon a cast,
> And he must run the hazard of the die."

Weary and miserable weeks they were, during which Earl Edmund waited the Pope's answer. It came at last. The Pope replied as only a Romish priest could be expected to reply. For the human anguish of the one he had no sympathy; for the quasi-religious sorrows of the other he had very much. He decreed, in the name of God, a full divorce between Edmund Earl of Cornwall, and Margaret his wife, coldly admonishing the Earl to take the Lord's chastening in good part, and to let the griefs of earth lift his soul towards Heaven.

But it was not there that this sorrow lifted it at first. The human agony had to be lived through before the Divine calm and peace could come to heal it. His last effort had been made in vain. The passionate hope of twenty years, that the day would come when his long, patient love should meet with its reward even on earth, was shattered to the dust. Even if she wished to come back after this, she could never retrace her steps. Compensation he might find in Heaven, but there could be none left for him on earth now. Even hope was dead within him.

The fatal Bull fell from the Earl's hand, and dropped a dead weight on the rushes at his feet. He was a heart-wrecked man, and life had to go on.

Was this man — for his is no fancy picture — a poor weak creature, or was he a strong, heroic soul? Many will write him down the weakling; perhaps all but those who have themselves known much of that hope deferred which maketh the heart sick, and drains away the moral life-blood drop by drop. It may be that the registers of Heaven held appended to his name a different epithet. It is harder to wait than to work; hardest of all to awake after long suspense to the blank conviction that all has been in vain, and then to take up the cross and meekly follow the Crucified.

Two hours later, a page brought a message to Reginald de Echingham to the effect that he was wanted by his master.

Reginald, in his own eyes, was a thoroughly miser-

able man. He had nobody to talk with, and nothing
to do. He missed Olympias sadly, for as the Earl
had once jestingly remarked, she burnt perpetual
incense on his altar, and flattery was a necessary
of life to Reginald. Olympias was the only person
who admired him nearly as much as he did himself
Like the old Romans, *panem et circenses* constituted
his list of indispensables; and had it been inevitable
to dispense with one of them for a time, Reginald
would have resigned the bread rather than the game.
On this particular morning, his basket of grievances
was full. The damp had put his moustache out of
curl; he had found a poor breakfast provided for
him—and Reginald was by no means indifferent to
his breakfast — and, worst of all, the mirror was
fixed so high up on the wall that he could not see
himself comfortably. The usual religious rites of
the morning before his own dear image had, therefore, to be very imperfectly performed. Reginald
grumbled sorely within himself as he went through
the cold stone passages which led to the Earl's
chamber.

His master lifted very sad eyes to his face.

"De Echingham, I wish to set out for Ashridge
to-morrow. Can you be ready?"

Ashridge! De Echingham would as soon have
received marching orders for Spitzbergen. If there
were one place in the world which he hated in his
inmost soul, it was that Priory in Buckinghamshire,
which Earl Edmund had himself founded. He would

be worse off there than even in Bermondsey Palace, with nothing around him but silent walls and almost equally silent monks. De Echingham ventured on remonstrance.

"Would not your Lordship find Berkhamsted much more pleasurable, especially at this season?"

"I do not want pleasure," answered the Earl wearily. "I want rest."

And he rose and began to walk aimlessly up and down the room, in that restless manner which was well suited to emphasise his words.

"But — your Lordship's pardon granted — would you not find it far better to seek for distraction and pleasance in the Court, than to shut yourself up in a gloomy cell with those monks?"

Earl Edmund stopped in his walk and looked at Reginald, whose speech touched his quick sense of humour.

"I would advise you to give thanks in your prayers to-night, De Echingham."

"For what, my Lord?"

"That you have as yet no conception of a sorrow which is past distraction by pleasance. 'Vinegar upon nitre!' You never tasted it, I should think."

"I thank your Lordship, I never did," said Reginald, who took the allusion quite literally.

"Well, I have done, and I did not like it," rejoined his master. "I prefer the monks' *soupe maigre*, if you please. Be so good as to make ready, De Echingham."

Reginald obeyed, but grumbling bitterly within his disappointed soul. Could there be any misery on earth worse than a cold stone bench, a bowl of sorrel soup, and a chapter of Saint Augustine to flavour it? And when they had only just touched the very edge of the London season! Why, he would not get a single ball that spring. Poor Reginald!

They stayed but one night at Berkhamsted, though, to the Earl, Berkhamsted was home. It was the scene of his birth, and of that blessed unapprehensive childhood, when brothers and sisters had played with him on the Castle green, and light, happy laughter had rung through the noble halls; when the hand of his fair Provençal mother had fallen softly in caresses on his head, and his generous, if extravagant, father had been only too ready to shower gold ducats in anticipation of his slightest wish. All was gone now but the cold gold—hard, silent, unfeeling; a miserable comforter indeed. There was one brother left, but he was far away—too far to recall in this desolate hour. Like a sufferer of later date, he must go alone with his God to bear his passion.[1]

The Priory of Ashridge—of the Order of Boni-Homines—which Earl Edmund had founded a few years before, was the only one of its class in England. The Predicant Friars were an offshoot of the Dominican Order; and the Boni-Homines were a

---

[1] "Je vais seul avec mon Dieu souffrir ma passion."—Bonnivard, Prior of St. Victor.

special division of the Predicant Friars. It is a singular fact that from this one source of Dominicans or Black Monks, sprang the best and the worst issues that ever emanated from monachism—the Boni-Homines and the Inquisition.

The Boni-Homines were, in a word, the Protestants of the Middle Ages. And—a remarkable feature—they were not, like all other seceders, persons who had separated themselves from the corruptions of Rome. They were better off, for they had never been tainted with them. From the first ages of primitive Christianity, while on all sides the stream was gradually growing sluggish and turbid, in the little nest of valleys between Dauphiné and Piedmont it had flowed fresh and pure, fed by the Word of God, which the Vaudois[1] mountaineers suffered no Pope nor Church to wrench or shut up from them.

The oldest name by which we know these early Protestants is Paulikians, probably having a reference to the Apostle Paul as either the exponent of their doctrines, or the actual founder of their local church. A little later we find them styled Cathari, or Pure Ones. Then we come on their third name of Albigenses, derived from the neighbouring town of Alby, where a Council was

---

[1] Vaudois is not really an accurate epithet, since the " Valley-Men " only acquired it when, in after years, ejected from their old home, they sought shelter in the Pays de Vaud. But it has come to be regarded as a name expressive of certain doctrines.

held which condemned them. But by whatever name they are called they are the same people, living in the same valleys, and holding unwaveringly and unadulterated the same faith.

It was by their fourth name of Boni-Homines, or Good Men, that they took advantage of the preaching movement set up by the Dominicans in the thirteenth century. They permeated their ranks, however, very gradually and quietly—perhaps all the more surely. For shortly after the date of this story, in the early part of the fourteenth century, it is said that of every three Predicant Friars, two were Boni-Homines.

The Boni-Homines were rife in France before they ever crept into England ; and the first man to introduce them into England was Edmund, Earl of Cornwall. A hundred years later, when the Boni-Homines had shown what they really were, and the leaven with which they had saturated society had evolved itself in Lollardism, the monks of other Orders did their best to bring both the movement and the men into disrepute, and to paint in the blackest colours the name of the Prince who had first introduced them into this country. In no monkish chronicle, unless written by a Bonus Homo, will the name of Earl Edmund be found recorded without some word of condemnation. And the Boni-Homines, unfortunately for history, were not much given to writing chronicles. Their business was saving souls.

Most important is it to remember, in forming just

L

estimates of the character of things—whether men
or events—in the Middle Ages, that with few exceptions monks were the only historians.   Before we can
truthfully set down this man as good, or that man as
bad, we must, therefore, consult other sources—the
chronicles of those few writers who were not monks,
the State papers, but above all, where accessible, the
personal accounts and private letters of the indivi-
duals in question.   It is pitiable to see well-mean-
ing Protestant writers, even in our own day, repeating
after each other the old monkish calumnies, and
never so much as pausing to inquire, Are these
things so ?

Late on the evening of the following day the Prior
and monks of Ashridge stood at the gate ready to
receive their founder.   The circumstances of his
coming were unknown to them, and they were prepared to make it a triumphal occasion.   But the
first glance at his face altered all that.   The Prior
quietly waved his monks back, and, going forward
himself, kissed his patron's hand, and led him silently
into the monastery.

Poor Sir Reginald found himself condemned to all
the sorrows he had anticipated, down to the sorrel
soup—for it was a vigil—and the straw mattress,
which, though considerably softer than the plank
beds of the monks, was barely endurable to his ease-
loving limbs.   He looked as he felt—extremely uncomfortable and exceedingly cross.

The Prior wasted no attentions on him.   Such

troubles as these were not worth a thought in his eyes; but his founder's face cost him many thoughts. He saw too plainly that for him had come one of those dread hours in life when the floods of deep waters overflow a man, and unless God take him into the ark of His covenant mercy, he will go down in the current. It was after some hours of prayer that the Prior tapped at the door of the royal guest.

Earl Edmund's quiet voice bade him enter.

" How fares it with my Lord ? "

" How is it likely to fare," was the sorrowful answer, " with one who hath lost hope ? "

The Prior sat down opposite his guest, where he might have the opportunity of studying his countenance. He was himself the senior of the Earl, being a man of about sixty years—a man in whom there had been a great deal of fire, and in whose dark, gleaming eyes there were many sparks left yet.

" Father," said the Earl, in a low, pained voice, " I am perplexed to understand God's dealings with me."

" Did you expect to understand them ? " was the reply.

" Thus far I did—that I thought He would finish what He had begun. But all my life—so far as this earthly life is concerned—I have been striving for one aim, and it has come to utter wreck. I set one object before me, and I thought—I *thought* it was God's will that I should pursue it. If He, by some act of His own providence. had shown me the contrary, I could have understood it better. But He has let men step in and spoil all. It is not He, but they who have brought about this wreck. My barge is not shattered by the winds and waves of God, but scuttled by the violence of pirates. My life is spoiled, and I do not understand why. I have done nothing but what I thought He intended me to do: I have set my heart on one thing, but it was a thing that I believed He meant to give me. It is all mystery to me."

"What is spoiled, my Lord? Is it what God meant you to do, or what you meant God to do?"

The sand grew to a larger heap in the hour-glass before another word was spoken.

"Father," said the Prince at last, "have I been intent on following my own will, when I thought I was pursuing the Lord's will for me? Father Bevis thinks so: he gave me some very hard words before I came here. He accuses me of idolatry; of loving the creature more than the Creator—nay, of setting up my will and aim, and caring nothing for those of the Lord. In his eyes, I ought to have perceived years ago that God called me to a life apart with Him, and to have detached my heart from all but Himself and His Church. Father, it is hard enough to realise the wreck of all a man hoped and longed for: yet it is harder to know that the very hope was sin, that the longing was contrary to the Divine purpose for me. Have I so misunderstood my life? Have I so misunderstood my Master?"

The expression of the Prior's eyes was very pitying and full of tenderness. Hard words were not what he thought needed as the medicine for that patient. They were only to be expected from Father Bevis, who had never suffered the least pang of that description of pain.

"My Lord," answered the Prior, gently, "it is written of the wicked man, 'Thou hast removed Thy judgments from his eyes.' They are not to be seen nor fathomed by him. And to a great extent it is equally true of the righteous man. Man must not look to be able to comprehend the ways of God— they are above him. It is enough for him if he can walk submissively in them."

"I wonder," said the Earl, still pursuing his own train of thought, "if I ought to have been a monk. I never imagined it, for I never felt any vocation. It seemed to me that Providence called me to a life entirely different. Have I made an utter blunder all my life? I cannot think it."

"There is no need to think it, my Lord. We cannot all be monks, even if we would. And why should we? It might, perhaps, be better for you to think one other thing."

"What?" asked the Earl, with more appearance of interest than he had hitherto shown.

"That what you suppose to be the spoiling of your life is just what God intended for you."

The Earl's face grew dark. "What! that all my life long He was leading me up to *this*?"

"It looks like it," said the Prior, quietly.

"Oh! but why?"

"Now, my Lord, you go beyond me. Neither you nor I can guess that. But He knows."

"Yes, I suppose He knows." But the consideration did not seem to comfort him as it had done before when suggested by Father Bevis.

"Perhaps," said the Prior again, softly, "there was no other way for your Lordship to the gate of the Holy City. He leads us by diverse ways; some through the flowery mead, and some over the desert sands where no water is. But of all it is written, 'He led them forth by the right way, that they might reach the haven of their desire.' Would your Lordship have preferred the mead and have missed the haven?"

"No," answered the Earl, firmly.

"Remember that you hold God's promise that when you awake up after His likeness you shall be satisfied with it. And he is not satisfied with his purchase who accounts it to have cost more than it was worth."

"Will your figure hold if pressed further?" said the Earl, with a wintry smile. "The purchase may be worth a thousand marks, but if I have but five hundred in the world I shall starve to death before the gem is mine."

"No, my Lord, it will not hold. For you cannot pay the price of that gem. The cost of it was His who will keep it safe for you, so that you cannot fling it away in mistake or folly. Figures must fail somewhere; and we want another in this case. My Lord, you are the gem, and the heavenly Graver is fashioning on you the King's likeness. Will you stay His hand before it is perfect?"

"I would it were near perfection!" sighed the Earl.

"Perhaps it is," said the Prior, gently. "Remember, it is your Father who is graving it."

The Earl's lip quivered. "If one could but know when it would be done! If one might know that in seven years—ten years—it would be complete, and one's heart and brain might find rest! But to think of its going on for twenty, thirty, forty——"

"They will look short enough, my Lord, when they are over."

"True. But not while they are passing."

"Nay, 'No-chastening for the present seemeth to be joyous.' Yet 'faint not when thou art rebuked of Him.'"

"It is the going on, that is so terrible!" said the Earl, almost under his breath. "If one might die when one's hope dies! Father, do you know anything of that?"

"In this world, my Lord, I dug a grave in mine own heart for all my hopes, forty years ago."

"And can you look back on that time calmly?"

"That depends on what you mean by calmness. Trustfully, yes; indifferently, no."

"Yet the religious say that God requires their

affections to be detached from the world. That must produce deadness of feeling."

"My Lord, there is such a thing as being alive from the dead. That is what God requires. If we tarry at the dying, we shall stop short of His perfection. We are to be dead to sin; but I nowhere find in Scripture that we are to die to love and happiness. That is man's gloss upon God's precept."

"Is that what you teach in your valleys?"

"We teach God's Word," said the Vaudois Prior. "Alas! for the men that have made it void through their tradition! 'If they speak not according thereunto, it is because there is no light in them.'"

"And you learn——" suggested the Earl in a more interested tone.

"We learn that God requires of His servants that they shall overcome the world; and He has told us what He means by the world—'The lust of the flesh, and the lust of the eyes, and the pride of life.' Whatever has become that to me, that am I to overcome, if I would reign with Christ when He cometh."

We Protestants can hardly understand the fearful extent to which Rome binds the souls of her votaries. When she goes so far—which she rarely does—as to hold out God's Word with one hand, she carries in the other an antidote to it which she calls the interpretation of the Church, derived from the consent of the Fathers. That the Fathers scarcely ever consent to anything does not trouble her. According to this interpretation, all human affection comes for monk or nun under the head of the lusts of the flesh.[1] A daughter's love for her mother, a father's for his child, is thus branded. From his cradle Earl Edmund had been taught this; was it any marvel if he found it impossible to get rid of the idea? The Prior's eyes were less blinded. He had come straight from those Piedmontese valleys where, from time immemorial, the Word of God has not been bound, and whosoever would has been free to slake his thirst at the pure fountain of the water of life. Love was not dead in his heart, and he was not ashamed of it.

"But then, Father, you must reckon all love a thing to be left behind?" very naturally queried the Earl.

"It will not be so in Heaven," answered the Prior; "then why should it be on earth? Left behind! Think you I left behind me the one love of my life when I became a Bonus Homo? I trow not. My Lord, forty years ago this summer, I was a young man, just entering life, and betrothed to a maiden of the Val Pellice. God laid His hand upon my hopes of earthly happiness, and said, 'Not so!' But must I, therefore, sweep my Adelaide's memory out

---

[1] "They (the Jesuits) were cut off from family and friends. Their vow taught them to forget their father's house, and to esteem themselves holy only when every affection and desire which nature had planted in their breasts had been plucked up by the roots." (*Jesuitism*, by the Rev. J. A. Wylie, LL.D.) This statement is simply a shade less true of the other monastic orders.

of my heart as if I had never loved her, and hold it sin against God to bear her sweet face in tender remembrance? Nay, verily, I have not so learned Christ."

"What happened?" said the Earl.

"God sent His angels for her," answered the Prior in a low voice.

"Ah, but she loved you!" was the response, in a tone still lower. The Earl did not know how much, in those few words, he told the Prior of Ashridge.

"My Lord," said the Prior, "did you ever purchase a gift for one you loved, and keep it by you, carefully wrapped up, not letting him know till the day came to produce it?"

The Earl looked up as if he did not see the object of the question; but he answered in the affirmative.

"It may be," continued the Prior, "that God our Father does the same at times. I believe that many will find gifts on their Father's table, at the great marriage-feast of the Lamb, which they never knew they were to have, and some which they fancied were lost irrevocably on earth. And if there be anything for which our hearts cry out that is not waiting for us, surely He can and will still the craving."

The Prior scarcely realised the effect of his words. He saw afterwards that the most painful part of the Earl's grief was lightened, that the terrible strain was gone from his eyes. He thanked God and took courage. He did not know that he had, to some extent, given him back the most precious thing he had lost—hope. He had only moved it further off—from earth to Heaven; and, if more distant, yet it was safer there.

The Prior left the Earl alone after that interview —alone with the Evangelisterium and the Psalter. The words of God were better for him than any words of men.

He stayed at Ashridge for about a fortnight, and then, to the ecstasy of Sir Reginald, issued orders for return to Berkhamsted. Only a few words passed between the Prior and his patron as they took leave of each other at the gate.

"Farewell, Father, and many thanks. You have done me good—as much good as man can do me now."

"My Lord, that acknowledgment is trust money, which I will pay into the treasury of your Lord and mine."

So they parted, to meet only once again. The Vaudois Prior was to go down with his friend to the river-side, to the last point where man can go with man.

CHAPTER X.

FORGIVENESS NOT TO BE FORGIVEN.

" Ay, there's a blank at my right hand
That ne'er can be made up to me."
—JAMES HOGG.

BEFORE leaving Bermondsey, the Earl had accomplished one of the hardest pieces of work which ever fell to his lot. This was the execution of the deed of separation which conveyed his legal assent to the departure of his wife, and assigned to her certain lands for her separate sustenance. Himself the richest man in England, he was determined that she should remain the wealthiest woman. He assigned to her all his lands in Norfolk and Suffolk, the manors of Kirketon in Lincolnshire, Malmesbury and Wyntreslawe in Wiltshire, and an annuity on Queenhithe, Middlesex—the whole sum amounting to £800 per annum, which was equivalent to at least £15,000 a year. He reserved to himself the appointments to all priories and churches, and the military feofs and escheats. Moreover, the Countess was not to sell any of the lands, nor had she the right to build castles. So far, in all probability, any man would have gone. But one other item was added, which came straight from the human heart of Earl Edmund, and was in the thirteenth century a very strange item indeed. The Countess, it was expressly provided, should not "waste, exile, enslave, nor destroy" the serfs on these estates.[1]

The soul of Haman the Agagite, which had descended upon Margaret de Clare, fiercely resented this unusual clause. On the same roll which contains the Earl's grant, in ordinary legal language— which must have cost him something where he records her wish, and his assent, "freely *during her widowhood* to dedicate herself to the service of God" —there is another document, in very extraordinary language, wherein the Lady Margaret recounts the wrongs which her lord is doing her in respect of this £800 a year. A more spiteful production was hardly ever penned. From the opening address "to all who shall read or hear this document" to the concluding assertion that she has hereto set her seal, the indenture is crammed full of envy, hatred, and malice, and all uncharitableness. She lets it plainly be seen that all the lands in Norfolk and Suffolk avail her nothing, so long as these restraining clauses are added to the grant. Margaret probably thought that she was merely detailing her wrongs; she did not realise that she was exhibiting her character. But for these four documents, the two letters, and the two indentures, wherein Earl and Countess have re-

---

[1] Rot. Pat., 22 Edw. I.

spectively " pressed their souls on paper," we might never have known which was to blame in the matter. Out of her own mouth is Margaret judged.

With amazing effrontery, and in flat contradiction not only of her husband's assertion, but of her own admission, the Countess commenced her tirade by bringing against her lord the charge of which she herself was guilty. As he was much the more worthy of credit, I prefer to believe him, confirmed as his statement is by her own letter to the Pope. She went on to detail the terms of separation, making the most of everything against her husband, and wound up with a sentence which must have pierced his heart like a poignard. She solemnly promised never to aggrieve him at any time by asking him to take her back, and never to seek absolution [1] from that oath! In one sentence of cold, cruel, concentrated spite, she sarcastically swore never to demand from him the love for which during one and twenty years he had sued to her in vain.

So now all was over between them. The worst that could come had come.

> " All was ended now, the hope, and the fear, and the sorrow,
>   All the aching heart, the restless unsatisfied longing,
>   All the dull deep pain, and constant anguish of patience ! "

There was no more left to fear, for there was nothing left to hope.

---

[1] The language of this sentence is remarkable :—" Jeo ou nul autre en moun noun purchace absolucion *ou de Apostoile ou de autre souerein.*" (Rot. Pat., 22 Edw. I.)

The Countess, attended by Father Miles and Felicia, left Rochester in June for Romsey Abbey, where she solemnly assumed the veil of a black nun. She was now plain Sister Margaret, and in due course of time and promotion, she would become Mother Margaret, and then, perhaps, Prioress and Abbess. And then—her soul would be required of her.

Mother Margaret! What bitter mockery of a title for the woman who had deliberately flung away from her as a worthless weed the white flower of love which she might have cherished!

Of course, the household was now scattered. Ada had been received into the household of the Countess of Gloucester, the King's daughter Joan. Olympias was pining to return to Reginald, if she could form some idea in what part of the world he might be found; Clarice was awaiting her imperious lord's commands. The morning after the Countess had taken her last farewell of them all, as they were still in this attitude of doubt and expectation, in walked Sir Lambert Aylmer. He was greeted with delight. Roisia was well, he reported, and sent her loving commendations to all; but the object of his coming was not to talk about Roisia. The Earl, with Sir Reginald, was at Restormel, one of his Cornish castles; but in a letter received from the latter gentleman, Sir Lambert had been requested to inform Olympias that their master desired them all to repair to Berkhamsted, whither he meant to come shortly, and they should then hear his intentions for the future.

"The saints send he mean not to be a monk!" said Olympias, shrugging her shoulders.

But nothing was further from Earl Edmund's purpose.

They reached Berkhamsted in a day or two, and to Clarice's great delight, found there not only Mistress Underdone and the two bower-maidens, but Sir Ademar and Heliet. It was a new and pleasant discovery that Heliet could travel. It had been a sort of accepted idea, never investigated, that her leaving Oakham was an impossibility; but Ademar had coaxed her to try, and Heliet was quite willing. The result was that she had reached Berkhamsted in safety, to her own intense enjoyment; for she had never before been a mile from Oakham, and the discovery that she was no longer a fixture, but could accompany her husband wherever duty called him, was to Heliet unspeakable delight.

It was not till October that the Earl reached home; for he stayed at Bristol for the wedding of the eldest princess, Alianora, with Henri Duke of Barre, which took place on the twentieth of September. The morning after his arrival he desired to speak with the whole of his household, who were to assemble in the hall for that purpose.

Olympias was positive that her master was about to take the cowl. "And it would be so nice, you see," she said; "just a match to the Lady."

"Nice, indeed!" said Reginald, pulling a terrible face. "Thou hast not spent a fortnight at Ashridge."

"Well, but he would not want to make a monk of thee," answered Olympias, rather blankly.

"He would not manage it, if he tried," responded her lord and master.

When the Earl's intentions were stated, it appeared that he had no further occasion for the services of Sir Reginald and Olympias, and he had secured for them situations, if they chose to accept them, in the household of the royal bride. Olympias was in ecstasies; to live in France was a most delicious fate in her eyes, nor did Reginald in the least object to it. Filomena and Sabina were provided for with the Countess of Lincoln and the Princess Elizabeth. Mistress Underdone, Heliet, and Sir Ademar would remain at Berkhamsted. And then the Earl, turning to Vivian and Clarice, requested as a favour to himself that they would remain also. It was necessary to have a lady of rank—namely, a knight's wife—at the head of the establishment. The Earl had no sister who could take that position; and his brother's widow, the Lady Constance d'Almayne, had preferred to return to her own home in Béarn rather than live in England. Heliet might have answered, but the Earl felt, with his usual considerate gentleness, that her lameness would make it a great charge and trouble to her. He wished Clarice to take it, if her husband would allow her, and was willing to continue in his service.

M

"And, truth to tell," said the Earl, with a sad smile at Rosie, who was making frantic efforts to compass the fearful distance of three yards between the Earl's chair and Clarice's outstretched hand, "you have here a jewel which I were very loth to lose from my empty casket. So, Sir Vivian, what say you?"

What became of either Clarice or Rosie was a matter of very little importance to Vivian, for he considered them both in the light of encumbrances—which was rather hard on Clarice at least, as she would thankfully have got out of his way if duty had allowed it. But, as he had once said, he knew when he was well off, and he had no wish to pass into the service either of a meaner nobleman or of a harder master. Vivian assented without a qualifying word.

Thus, with Clarice, life sank back into its old groove, and time sped on, uneventful except for the two items that every day little Rosie grew in intelligence and attractiveness, and every month, as it seemed to her mother, the Earl grew a year older. Clarice doubted if Rosie were not his sole tie to life. She became his chief companion, and on the little child who was no kin of his he poured out all the rich treasure of that warm great heart which his own held at so small a value. Rosie, however, was by no means irresponsive. Any one seeing her would have taken the Earl to be her father, and Sir Vivian a stranger of whom she was rather frightened.

The year 1294 was signalised by a remarkable action on the part of King Edward. In order to defray the vast expenses of his Welsh and Breton wars, he took into his own hands all the priories in England, committing their lands and goods to the care of state officials, and allowing eighteenpence per week for the sustenance of each monk. The allowance was handsome, but the proceeding was very like burglary.

The exact religious position of Edward the First is not so easy to define as that of some other monarchs. With respect to any personal and spiritual religion, it is, alas! only too easy. But it is difficult to say how far his opposition to the Pope originated from a deliberate policy, well thought out beforehand, and how far from the momentary irritation of a crossed will. He certainly was not the intelligent supporter of the Boni-Homines from personal conviction, that was to be found in his son, Edward II., or in his cousin, Edmund, Earl of Cornwall. Yet he did support them to a certain extent, though more in the earlier part of his life than in the later. Like many another man in his position, he was ready enough to assist a body of sensible literary reformers, but, when the doctrine which they held began to press personally on himself, he shrank from the touch of Ithuriel's spear. That his subjects should be made better and more obedient by means of the Decalogue, or any other code, was a most excellent thing ; but when the Decalogue came closer and said, " Thou shalt not," to himself, then it was an intrusive nuisance.

In the following year, 1295, the King laid the foundation of borough representation, by directing the sheriffs of the various counties to send to Parliament, along with the knights of the shire, two deputies from each borough, who were to be elected by the townsmen, and empowered to consent, in the name of their constituents, to the decrees of the King and his Council. "It is a most equitable rule," added the Monarch, "that what concerns all should be judged of by all." Concerning the possibility of these members dissenting from his decrees, however, His Majesty was not quite so eloquent. That contingency was one which a sovereign in the thirteenth century could scarcely be expected to take into his august consideration.

But King Edward wanted more money, and apparently preferred to grind it out of his monks rather than his peasants. He now instituted a search of all the monasteries in England, and commanded the confiscation of all cash. The monasteries resisting the excessive taxation laid upon them, the King seized their lay fees.

In the December of this year, Earl Edmund left Berkhamsted for Cornwall, taking with him Vivian, and leaving Ademar behind as the only gentleman in the party. He was going on an errand unpleasant to himself, for the King had committed to his charge a portion of the Gascon army. War and contention were altogether out of his line, yet he had no choice but to obey. He joined his cousin, the Earl of Lancaster, and the Earl of Lincoln, in Cornwall, and together they sailed on the fifteenth of January 1296, from a Cornish port termed Plumhupe in the "Chronicle of Worcester," but not easy to identify now, unless it be taken as a blunder for Plymouth, and the chronicler be supposed ignorant of its county. With them were twenty-five barons and a thousand knights.

During the absence of the Earl, it struck his cousin, the King—for no other reason can be guessed —that the Earl's treasury being much better filled than his own, he might reasonably pay his debts out of his cousin's overflowing coffers. Accordingly he sent to Berkhamsted, much to the dismay of the household, and coolly annexed his cousin's valuables to the Crown. But Earl Edmund was a man in whose eyes gold was of comparatively small value, partly because he set other things much higher, and partly because he had always had so much of it, that poverty was a trouble which he was scarcely able to realise.

A sad year was 1296 to the royal family of England. The Gascon expedition proved so disastrous, that Edmund, Earl of Lancaster, died of grief and disappointment at Bayonne on the fifth of June; and the Scottish one, though brilliantly successful in a political light, cost no less, for an arrow shot at a venture, at the siege of Berwick, quenched the young life of Richard Plantagenet, the only brother and last near relation of Edmund, Earl of Cornwall. The triumphant capture of the coronation chair and the Stone of Destiny and their removal from Dunstaffnage to England, was contrasted with a terrible famine, which so affected the vines in particular, that there was hardly wine enough left for mass.

In the midst of these sharp contrasts of triumph and sorrow, Earl Edmund returned to England, escorting his widowed cousin Queen Blanche, and following the coffin of the Earl of Lancaster. They found the King earnestly engaged in effecting a contract of marriage between the young Prince Edward and a daughter of Guy, Count of Flanders, and binding himself to march to Guy's assistance against the King of France.

Ah, had it been God's will that the wife destined for Edward II. should have been the pure, high-minded, heroic Philippine of Flanders, instead of the she-wolf of France, what a different history he would have had!

For among all the princesses of the thirteenth century one of the fairest souls is this Flemish maiden, who literally laid down her life in ransom for her father. It was not Prince Edward's fault that Philippine was not Queen of England. It was the fault of the ambitious policy alike of King Edward and the King of France, and perhaps still more of his Navarrese Queen. They did not know that they were sacrificing not only Philippine, but Edward. Would they have cared much about it if they had done?

The regalia of Scotland were solemnly offered at the shrine of St. Edward on the 17th of June. Earl Edmund was present at the ceremony, and after it, "weary with the storms of earth," he went home to court repose at Berkhamsted.

It was the day after he came home, a soft, warm June day. Clarice and Heliet were playing with Rosie, now a bright, lively little child of five years old. In rushing away from Heliet, who was pretending to catch her, Rosie, to the dismay of all parties, ran straight against her father, who had just reached the top of the spiral staircase which led to their own rooms. Vivian, never very amiable when his course was impeded, either by a physical or a moral hindrance, impatiently pushed the child on one side. It was the wrong side. Rosie struggled to recover her balance for one moment, during which her father's hand *might* have grasped her, had he been quick to do it; her mother had not time to reach her. Then, with an inarticulate cry for help, she went down the well of the staircase.

Past Heliet's exclamation of horror came a sharp ringing shriek—"O Vivian! Rosie!" and darting by her astounded husband, down the stairs fled Clarice, with a celerity that she would have thought impossible an hour before.

Vivian's state of mind was a mixture of selfishness and horror. He had not intended to hurt the child, merely to get her out of his way; but when selfishness and remorse struggle together, the worse of the two usually comes to the front. Vivian's first articulate answer was a growl at his wife.

"Why did you not keep her out of my way? Gramercy, what a fuss about a girl!"

Then he read his guilt in Heliet's eyes, and began

faltering out excuses and asseverations that he had not meant anything.

Clarice reached the foot of the stairs without heeding a word he said. But other hands, as tender as her own, were there before her.

"Little Rosie! my poor little child!" came from Earl Edmund's gentle lips, as he lifted the bruised child in his arms. Tenderly as it was done, Rosie could not repress a moan of pain which went to the two hearts that loved her.

She was not killed, but she was dying.

"A few hours," said the Earl's physician, instantly summoned, "a few hours. There was nothing to be done. She would very likely not suffer much—would hardly be conscious of pain until the end came."

The Earl bore her into his own chamber, and laid her on his bed. With speechless agony Clarice watched beside her.

Just once Rosie spoke.

"Mother, Mother, don't cry!"

Clarice was shedding no tears; they would not come yet; but in Rosie's eyes her strained white face was an equivalent.

"Mother, don't cry," said Rosie. "You said—I asked you—why people died. You said our Lord called them. Must go—when our Lord calls."

Clarice was not able to answer; but Rosie's words struck cold to her heart.

"Must go when our Lord calls!"

She could hardly pray. What went up was not

prayer, but rather a wild, passionate cry that this thing could not be—should not be.

There were those few hours of half-consciousness, and then, just at the turn of the night, the Lord came and called, and Rosie heard His voice, and went to Him.

Sir Vivian Barkeworth, during that day and night, was not pursuing the even tenor of his way in that state of complacent self-approval which was the usual attitude of his mind. It was not that he mourned the child; his affections were at all times of a microscopic character, and the only spark of regard which he entertained for Rosie was not as his little child, but as his future heiress. Nor was he at all troubled by the sufferings of Clarice. Women were always crying about something; they were decided hindrances and vexations in a man's way; in fact, the existence of women at all, except to see to a man's comforts, and amuse his leisure, was, in Sir Vivian's eyes, an unfortunate mistake in the arrangements of Providence. He mourned first the good opinion which people had of him, and which, by the way, was a much smaller package than Sir Vivian thought it; and secondly, the far more important disturbance of the excellent opinion which he had of himself. He could not rid himself of the unpleasant conviction that a little more patience and amiability on his part would have prevented all this disagreeable affair, though he would not for the world have acknowledged this conviction to Clarice. That was

what he thought it—a disagreeable affair. It was
the purest accident, he said to himself, and might
have happened to any one. At the same time, something, which did not often trouble Vivian, deep down
in his inner man, distinctly told him that such an
accident would never have happened to the Earl or
Sir Ademar. Vivian only growled at his conscience
when it gave him that faint prick. He was so accustomed to bid it be quiet, that it had almost ceased
to give him any hints, and the pricking was very
slight.

"A disagreeable business!" he said, inwardly;
"a most disagreeable business. Why did not Clarice
attend to her duties better? It was her duty to keep
that child from bothering me. What are women
good for but to keep their children out of mischief,
and to see that their husbands' paths through life
are free from every thorn and pebble?"

Sir Vivian had reached this point when one of the
Earl's pages brought him a message. His master
wished his attendance in his private sitting-room.
Vivian inwardly anathematised the Earl, the page,
Heliet (as a witness), Rosie (as the offender), but
above all, as the head and front of all his misery,
Clarice. He was not the less disposed to anathemas
when he found Sir Ademar, Heliet, Clarice, and
Master Franco, the physician, assembled to receive
him with the Earl. It rasped him further to perceive
that they were all exceedingly grave, though how he
could have expected any of them to look hilarious it

would be difficult to say. Especially he resented the look of desolate despair in Clarice's eyes, and the physical exhaustion and mental agony written in every line of her white face. He would not have liked to admit that he felt them all as so many trumpet-tongued accusers against him.

"I desired you all to assemble," said the Earl, in tones as gentle as usual, but with an under-current of pain, "because I wish to inquire in what manner our poor little darling met her death. How came she to fall down the staircase?"

He looked at Heliet, and she was the one to reply.

"It was an accident, my Lord, I think," she said.

"'You think?' Is there some doubt, then?"

No one answered him but Ademar. "Pardon me, my Lord; I was not present."

"Then I ask one who was present. Dame Heliet?"

"I hope there is no doubt, my Lord," answered Heliet. "I should be sorry to think so."

The bushy eyebrows, which were the only blemish to the handsome Plantagenet face of the Earl, were lowered at this reply.

"What am I to understand by that?" he asked. "Did the child throw herself down of her own will?"

"Oh, no, my Lord, no!"

"Did any one push her down?"

Dead silence.

"Sir Ademar was not present. Were you, Sir Vivian?"

Vivian, whose face was far more eloquent in this instance than his tongue, muttered an affirmative.

"Then you can answer me. Did any one push her down?"

Vivian's reply was unintelligible, being hardly articulate.

"Will you have the goodness to repeat that, if you please?" said his master.

In Clarice's heart a terrible tempest had been raging. Ought she not to speak, and declare the fact of which she felt sure, that Vivian had not been intentionally the murderer of his child? that whatever he might have done, he had meant no more than simply to push her aside? Conscientiousness strove hard with bitterness and revenge. Why should she go out of her way to shield the man who had been the misery of her life from the just penalty which he deserved for having made that life more desolate than ever? She knew that her voice would be the most potent there—that her vote would outweigh twenty others. The pleading of the bereaved mother in favour of the father of the dead child was just what would make its way straight to the heart of his judge. Clarice's own heart said passionately, No! Rosie's dead face must stand between him and her for ever. But then upon her spirit's fever fell calming words—words which she repeated every day of her life—words which she had taught Rosie.

"Forgive us our debts, as we forgive our debtors."

If God were to forgive her as she forgave Vivian,

what would become of her? Would she ever see
Rosie again? And then a cry for help and strength
to do it went up beyond the stars.

The Earl was quietly waiting for the repetition of
Vivian's answer. It came at last—the answer—not
a repetition.

"St. Mary love us, my Lord! I never meant any
harm."

"You never meant!" replied a stern voice, not at all
like Earl Edmund's gentle tones. "Did you *do* it?"

Before Vivian could reply, to every one's astonishment, and most of all to his, Clarice threw herself
down on her knees, and deprecatingly kissed the
hand which rested on the arm of her master's chair.

"Mercy, my good Lord, I entreat you! It was
a pure accident, and nothing more. I know Sir
Vivian meant no more than to push the child
gently out of his way. He did not calculate on
the force he used. It was only an accident—he
never thought of hurting her. For the sake of my
dead darling, whom I know you loved, my gracious
Lord, grant me mercy for her father!"

The silence was broken for a moment only by
Heliet's sobs. The Earl had covered his face with
his hands. Then he looked into Clarice's pleading
eyes, with eyes in which unshed tears were glistening.

"Dame Clarice," said Earl Edmund in his softest
tone, "*you* wish me to grant Sir Vivian mercy?"

"I implore it of your Lordship, for His sake to
whom my child is gone, and hers."

The Earl's eyes went to Vivian, who stood looking the picture of guilt and misery.

"You hear, Sir Vivian? You are pardoned, but not for your sake. Be it yours to repay this generous heart."

The party dispersed in a few minutes. But when Ademar and Heliet found themselves alone, the former said—"Will he love her after this?"

"Love her!" returned Heliet. "My dear husband, thou dost not know that man. He owes his life to her generosity, and he will never forgive her for it."

CHAPTER XI.

THE SUN BREAKS OUT.

"If from Thine ordeal's heated bars,
Our feet are seamed with crimson scars,
Thy will be done!"—WHITTIER.

ELIET'S penetration had not deceived her. The mean, narrow, withered article which Vivian Barkeworth called his soul, was unable to pardon Clarice for having shown herself morally so much his superior. That his wife should be better than himself was in his eyes an inversion of the proper order of things. And as of course it was impossible that he should be to blame, why, it must be her fault. Clarice found herself most cruelly snubbed for days after her interference in behalf of her graceless husband. Not in public; for except in the one instance of this examination, where his sense of shame and guilt had overcome him for a moment, Vivian's company manners were faultless, and a surface observer would have pronounced him a model husband. Poor Clarice had learned by experience that any restraint which Vivian put upon himself when inwardly vexed, was sure to rebound on her devoted head in the form of after suffering in private.

To Clarice herself the reaction came soon and severely.   On the evening before Rosie's funeral, Heliet found her seated by the little bier in the hall, gazing dreamily on the face of her lost darling, with dry eyes and strained expression.   She sat down beside her.   Clarice took no notice.   Heliet scarcely knew how to deal with her.   If something could be said which would set the tears flowing it might save her great suffering ; yet to say the wrong thing might do more harm than good.   The supper-bell rang before she had made up her mind.   As they rose Clarice slipped her hand into Heliet's arm, and, to the surprise of the latter, thanked her.

" For what ? " said Heliet.

" For the only thing any one can do for me—for feeling with me."

After supper Clarice went up to her own rooms; but Heliet returned to the hall where Rosie lay.   To her astonishment, she found a sudden and touching change in the surroundings of the dead child.   Rosie lay now wreathed round in white rosebuds, tastefully disposed, as by a hand which had grudged neither love nor labour.

" Who has done this ? " Heliet spoke aloud in her surprise.

" I have," said a voice beside her.   It was no voice

which Heliet knew. She looked up into the face of
a tall man, with dark hair and beard, and eyes which
were at once sad and compassionate.

"You! Who are you?" asked Heliet in the same
tone.

"You may not know my name. I am—Piers
Ingham."

"Then I do know," replied Heliet, gravely. "But,
Sir Piers, *she* must not know."

"Certainly not," he said, quietly. "Tell her
nothing; let her think, if she will, that the angels did
it. And—tell me nothing. Farewell."

He stooped down and kissed the cold white brow
of the dead child.

"That can hurt no one," said Piers, in a low voice.
"And she may be glad to hear it—when she meets
the child again."

He glided out of the hall so softly that Heliet did
not hear him go, and only looked up and found herself alone. She knelt for a few minutes by the bier,
and then went quietly to her own room.

The next morning there were abundance of con-
jectures as to who could have paid this tender and
graceful tribute. The Earl was generally suspected,
but he at once said that it was no doing of his.
Everybody was asked, and all denied it. Father
Bevis was appealed to, as being better acquainted
with the saints than the rest of the company, to state
whether he thought it probable that one of them had
been the agent. But Father Bevis's strong common

N

sense declined to credit any but human hands with
the deed.

Clarice was one of the last to appear. And when
the sweet, fair tribute to her darling broke suddenly
upon her sight, the result was attained for which all
had been more or less hoping. That touch of nature
set the floodgates open, and dropping on her knees
beside the bier, Clarice poured forth a rain of passionate tears.

When all was over, and Rosie had been hidden
away from sight until the angel-trump should call
her, Clarice and Heliet went out together on the
Castle green. They sat down on one of the seats in
an embrasure. The Earl, with his thoughtful kindness, seeing them, sent word to the commandant to
keep the soldiers within so long as the ladies chose to
stay there. So they were left undisturbed.

Heliet was longing intensely to comfort Clarice,
but she felt entirely at a loss what line to take.
Clarice relieved her perplexity by being the first to
speak.

"Heliet!" she said, "what does God mean by
this?"

"I cannot tell, dear heart, except that He means
love and mercy. 'All the ways of the Lord are
mercy and truth unto the lovers of His will and testimony.' Is not that enough?"

"It might be if one could see it."

"Is it not enough, without seeing?"

"O Heliet, Heliet, she was all I had!"

"I know it, beloved. But how if He would have thee to make Him all thou hast?"

"Could I not have loved God and have had Rosie?"

"Perhaps not," said Heliet, gently.

"I hope He will take me soon," said Clarice. "Surely He can never leave me long now!"

"Or, it may be, make thee content to wait His will."

Clarice shook her head, not so much with a negative air as with a shrinking one. Just in that first agony, to be content with it seemed beyond human nature.

Heliet laid her hand on that of her friend. "Dear, would you have had Rosie suffer as you have done?"

For a moment Clarice's mental eyes ran forward, over what would most likely, according to human prevision, have been the course of Rosie's after life. The thought came to her as with a pang, and grew upon her, that the future could have had no easy lot in store for Vivian Barkeworth's daughter. He would have disposed of her without a thought of her own wish, and no prayers nor tears from her would have availed to turn him from his purpose. No—it was well with the child.

"Thou art right," she said, in a pained voice. "It is better for Rosie as it is. But for me?"

"Leave that with God, He will show thee some day that it was better for thee too."

Clarice rose from her seat; but not till she had

said the one thing which Heliet had been hoping that she would not say.

"Who could have laid those flowers there? Heliet, canst thou form any idea? Dost thou think it *was* an angel?"

Heliet had an excuse in settling her crutches for delaying her reply for a moment. Then she said in a low tone, the source of whose tenderness it was well that Clarice could not guess—"I am not sure, dear, that it was not."

If Clarice's sufferings had been passive before, they began to be active now. Vivian made her life a torment to her by jealousy on the one hand, and positive cruelty on the other; yet his manners in public were so carefully veiled in courtesy that not one of her friends guessed how much she really suffered. As much time as she could she spent in her oratory, which was the only place where Vivian left her at peace, under a vague idea that it would bring him ill luck to interrupt any one's prayers. Unfortunately for Clarice, he had caught a glimpse of Piers, and, having no conscientiousness in his own composition, he could not imagine it in that of another. That Piers should be at Berkhamsted without at least making an effort to open communication with Clarice, was an idea which Vivian would have refused to entertain for a moment. For what other earthly purpose could he be there? Vivian was a man who had no faith in any human being. In his belief, the only possible means to prevent Clarice from running away with Piers was to keep her either in his sight or locked up when out of it. The idea of trusting to her principles would have struck him as simply ridiculous.

Sir Piers, however, had completely disappeared, as completely as though he had never been seen. And after a while Vivian grew more confident, and not so particular about keeping the key turned. Clarice knew neither why he locked her in, nor why he gave over doing so. Had she had a suspicion of the reason, her indignation would not have been small.

Public affairs meanwhile maintained their interest. The King marched his army to Scotland, and routed Wallace's troops in the battle of Falkirk; but his success was somewhat counterbalanced by the burning of Westminster Palace and Abbey before he left home. It was about this time that Piers Gavestone began to appear at Court, introduced by his father with a view to making his fortune; and to the misfortune of the young Prince Edward, their musical tastes being alike, they became fast friends. The Prince was now only fourteen years of age; and, led by Gavestone, he was guilty—if indeed the charge be true—of a mischievous boyish frolic, in "breaking the parks" of the Bishop of Chester, and appropriating his deer. The boy was fond of venison, and he was still more fond of pets; but neither of these facts excused the raid on the Bishop of

Chester, who chose to take the offence far more seriously than any modern bishop would be likely to do, and carried his complaint to the King. The royal father, as his wont was, flew into a passion, and weighted the boys' frolic with the heavy penalty of banishment for Gavestone, and imprisonment for the Prince. In all probability young Edward had never looked on his action in any other light than as a piece of fun. Had his father been concerned about the sin committed against God—exactly the sin of a boy who robs an orchard—he might, with less outward severity, have produced a far more wholesome impression on his son; but what he considered appears to have been merely the dignity of the Prince, which was outraged by the act of the boy who bore the title. A quiet, grave exhortation might have done him good, but imprisonment did none, and left on many minds the impression that the boy had been hardly used.

One striking feature in the conduct of Edward II. is the remarkable meekness and submission with which he bore his father's angry outbursts and severe punishments — often administered for mere youthful follies, such as most fathers would think amply punished by a strong lecture, and perhaps a few strokes of the cane. Edward I. seems to have been one of those men who entirely forget their own childhood, and are never able in after life to enter into the feelings of a child.

His Majesty, however, had other matters to attend

to beside the provocation received from his heir; for in the month of September following (1299) he was married at Canterbury to the Princess Marguerite of France. It was a case approaching that of Rachel and Leah, for it was the beautiful Princess Blanche for whom the King had been in treaty, and Marguerite was foisted on him by a process of crafty diplomacy not far removed from treachery. However, since Marguerite, though not so fair as her sister, proved the better woman of the two, the King had no reason to be disappointed in the end.

The Council of Regency established in Scotland, discontented with Edward's arbitration, referred the question of their independence to the Pope, and that wily potentate settled the matter in his own interests, by declaring Scotland a fief of the Holy See. The King was still warring in that vicinity; the young Queen was left with her baby boy in Yorkshire to await his return.

It was a hot July day, and Vivian, who highly disapproved of the stagnation of Berkhamsted, declared his intention of going out to hunt. People hunted in all weathers and seasons in the Middle Ages. Ademar declined to accompany him, and he contented himself by taking two of the Earl's squires and a handful of archers as company. The Earl did not interfere with Vivian's proceedings. He was quite aware that the quiet which he loved was by no means to everybody's taste; and he left his retinue at liberty to amuse themselves as they pleased.

Vivian did not think it necessary to turn the key on Clarice; but he gave her a severe lecture on discreet behaviour which astonished her, since her conscience did not accuse her of any breach of that virtue, and she could not trace the course of her husband's thoughts. Clarice meekly promised to bear the recommendation in mind; and Vivian left her to her own devices.

The day dragged heavily. Mistress Underdone sat with Heliet and Clarice at work; but not much work was gone through, for in everybody's opinion it was too hot to do anything. The tower in which they were was at the back of the Castle, and looked upon the inner court. The Earl's apartments were in the next tower, and there, despite the heat, he was going over sundry grants and indentures with Father Bevis and his bailiff, always considering the comfort and advantage of his serfs and tenants. The sound of a horn outside warned the ladies that in all probability Vivian was returning home; and whether his temper were good, bad, or indifferent was likely to depend on the condition of his hunting-bags. Good, was almost too much to hope for. With a little smothered sigh Clarice ventured to hope that it might not be worse than indifferent. Her comfort for the next day or two would be much affected by it.

They looked out of the window, but all they saw was Ademar crossing the inner court with rapid steps, and disappearing within the Earl's tower. There was some noise in the outer court, but no discernible solution of it. The ladies went back to their work. Much to their surprise, ten minutes later, the Earl himself entered the chamber. It was not at all his wont to come there. When he had occasion to send orders to Clarice concerning his household arrangements, he either sent for her or conveyed them through Vivian. These were the Countess's rooms which they were now occupying, and the Earl had never crossed the threshold since she left the Castle.

They looked up, and saw in his face that he had news to tell them. And all at once Clarice rose and exclaimed—"Vivian!"

"Dame, I grieve to tell you that your knight has been somewhat hurt in his hunting."

Clarice was not conscious of any feeling but the necessity of knowing all. And that she had not yet been told all she felt certain.

"Much hurt?" she asked.

"I fear so," answered the Earl.

"My Lord, will you tell me all?"

The Earl took her hand and looked kindly at her. "Dame, he is dead."

Mistress Underdone raised her hands with an exclamation of shocked surprise, to which Heliet's look of horror formed a fitting corollary. Clarice was conscious only of a confused medley of feelings, from which none but a sense of amazement stood out in the foreground. Then the Earl quietly told her that, in leaping a wide ditch, Vivian had been thrown from his horse, and had never spoken more.

No one tried to comfort Clarice. Pitifully they all felt that comfort was not wanted now. The death of Rosie had been a crushing blow; but Vivian's, however sudden, could hardly be otherwise than a relief. The only compassion that any one could feel was for him, for whom there was

> "No;reckoning made, but sent to his account
> With all his imperfections on his head."

The very fact that she could not regret him on her own account lay a weight on Clarice's conscience, though it was purely his own fault. Severely as she tried to judge herself, she could recall no instance in which, so far as such a thing can be said of any human sinner, she had not done her duty by that dead man. She had obeyed him in letter and spirit, however distasteful it had often been to herself; she had consulted his wishes before her own; she had even honestly tried to love him, and he had made it impossible. Now, she could not resist the overwhelming consciousness that his death was to her a release from her fetters—a coming out of prison. She was free from the perpetual drag of apprehension on the one hand, and of constantly endeavouring on the other to please a man who was determined not to be pleased. The spirit of the uncaged bird awoke within her—a sense of freedom, and light, and rest, such as she had not known for those eight weary years of her married slavery.

Yet the future was no path of roses to the eyes of Clarice. She was not free in the thirteenth century, in the sense in which she would have been free in the nineteenth, for she had no power to choose her own lot. All widows were wards of the Crown; and it was not at all usual for the Crown to concern its august self respecting their wishes, unless they bought leave to comply with them at a very costly price. By a singular perversion of justice, the tax upon a widow who purchased permission to remarry or not, at her pleasure, was far heavier than the fine exacted from a man who married a ward of the Crown without royal licence. The natural result of this arrangement was that the ladies who were either dowered widows or spinster heiresses very often contracted clandestine marriages, and their husbands quietly endured the subsequent fine and imprisonment, as unavoidable evils which were soon over, and well worth the advantage which they purchased.

It seemed, however, as if blessings, no less than misfortunes, were not to come single to Clarice Barkeworth. A few weeks after Vivian's death, the Earl silently put a parchment into her hand, which conveyed to her the information that King Edward had granted to his well-beloved cousin, Edmund, Earl of Cornwall, the marriage of Clarice, widow of Vivian Barkeworth, knight, with the usual proviso that she was not to marry one of the King's enemies. This was, indeed, something for which to be thankful. Clarice knew that her future was as safe in her master's hands as in her own.

"Ah!" said Heliet, when that remark was made to her, "if we could only have felt, dear heart, that it was as safe in the hands of his Master!"

"Was I very faithless, Heliet?" said Clarice, with tears in her eyes.

"Dear heart, no more than I was!" was Heliet's answer.

"But has it not occurred to thee, Heliet, now— why might I not have had Rosie?"

"I know not, dear Clarice, any more than Rosie knew, when she was a babe in thine arms, why thou gavest her bitter medicine. Oh, leave all that alone —our Master understands what He is doing."

It was the middle of September, and about two months after Vivian's death. Clarice sat sewing, robed in the white weeds of widowhood, in the room which she usually occupied in the Countess's tower. The garments worn by a widow were at this time extremely strict and very unbecoming, though the period during which they were worn was much less stringent than now. From one to six months was as long as many widows remained in that condition. Heliet had not been seen for an hour or more, and Mistress Underdone, with some barely intelligible remarks very disparaging to "that Nell," who stood, under her, at the head of the kitchen department, had disappeared to oversee the venison pasty. Clarice was doing something which she had not done for eight years, though hardly aware that she was doing it—humming a troubadour song. Getting past an awkward place in her work, words as well as music became audible—

> "And though my lot were hard and bare,
> And though my hopes were few,
> Yet would I dare one vow to swear—
> My heart should still be true."

"Wouldst thou, Clarice?" asked a voice behind her.

Clarice's delicate embroidery got the worst of it, for it dropped in a heap on the rushes, and nobody paid the slightest attention to it for a considerable time. Nor did any one come near the room until Heliet made her appearance, and she came so slowly, and heralded her approach by such emphatic raps of her crutches on the stone floor, that Clarice could scarcely avoid the conclusion that she was a conspirator in the plot. The head and front of it all, however, was manifestly Earl Edmund, who received Sir Piers with a smile and no other greeting—a distinct intimation that it was not the first time they had met that day.

The wedding—which nobody felt inclined to dispute—was fixed for the fifteenth of October. The Earl wished it to take place when he could be present and give away the bride, and he wanted first a fortnight's retreat at Ashridge, to which place he had arranged to go on the last day of September. Sir Piers stepped at once into his old position, but the

Earl took Ademar with him to Ashridge. He gave
the grant of Clarice's marriage to Piers himself, in
the presence of the household, with the remark :—

"It will be better in your hands than mine; and
there is no time like the present."

Into Clarice's hand her master put a shining pile
of gold for the purchase of wedding garments and
jewellery.

"I am glad," he said, "that your path through life
is coming to the roses now.   I would hope the thorns
are over for you—at least for some time.   There have
been no roses for me; but I can rejoice, I hope, with
those for whom they blossom."

And so he rode away from Berkhamsted, looking
back to smile a farewell to Heliet and Clarice, as
they stood watching him in the gateway.   Long
years afterwards they remembered that kind, almost
affectionate, smile.

As the ladies turned into their own tower, and
began to ascend the staircase—always a slow process with Heliet—Clarice said, "I cannot understand
why our Lord the Earl has such a lonely and sorrowful lot."

"Thou wouldst like to understand everything,
Clarice," returned Heliet, smiling.

"I would!" she answered.   "I can understand my
own troubles better, for I know how much there is
in me that needs setting right; but he—why he is
almost an angel already."

"Perhaps he would tell thee the same thing," said

Heliet. "I am afraid, dear heart, if thou hadst the graving of our Lord's gems, thou wouldst stop the tool before the portrait was in sufficient relief."

"But when the portrait *is* in sufficient relief?" answered Clarice, earnestly.

"Ah, dear heart!" said Heliet, "neither thine eyes nor mine are fine enough to judge of that."

"It seems almost a shame to be happy when I know he is not," replied Clarice, the tears springing to her eyes; "our dear master, who has been to me as a very angel of God."

"Nay, dear, he would wish thee to be happy," gently remonstrated Heliet. "I believe both thou and I are to him as daughters, Clarice."

"I wish I could make him happy!" said Clarice, as they turned into her rooms.

"Ask God to do it," was Heliet's response.

They both asked Him that night. And He heard and answered them, but, as is often the case, not at all as they expected.

CHAPTER XII.

IN THE CITY OF GOLD.

> "I am not eager, strong,
>   Nor bold—all that is past;
> I am ready not to do,
>   At last—at last.
>
> "My half-day's work is done,
>   And this is all my part :
> I give a patient God
>   My patient heart."

VESPERS were over at Ashridge on the last day of September, the evening of the Earl's arrival. He sat in the guest-chamber, with the Prior and his Buckinghamshire bailiff, to whom he was issuing instructions with respect to some cottages to be built for the villeins on one of his estates. The Prior sat by in silence, while the Earl impressed on the mind of his agent that the cottages were to be made reasonably comfortable for the habitation of immortal souls and not improbably suffering bodies. When at last the bailiff had departed, the Prior turned to his patron with a smile. "I would all lay lords—and spiritual ones too—were as kindly thoughtful of their inferiors as your Lordship."

"Ah, how little one can do at the best!" said the Earl. "Life is full of miseries for these poor serfs; shall we, who would follow Christ's steps, not strive to lighten it?"

"It is very truth," said the Prior.

"Ay, and how short the boundary is!" pursued the Earl. "'Man is ignorant what was before him; and what shall be after him, who can tell him?' It may be, the next lord of these lands will be a hard man, who will oppress his serfs, or at any rate take no care for their comfort. Poor souls! let them be happy as long as they can."

"When I last saw your Lordship, you seemed to think that short boundary too long for your wishes."

"It is seven years since that," answered the Earl. "It hardly seems so far away now. And lately, Father—I scarcely can tell how—I have imagined that my life will not be long. It makes me the more anxious to do all I can ere 'the night cometh in which no man can work.'"

The Prior looked critically and anxiously at his patron. The seven years which he had passed in sorrowful loneliness had aged him more than seven years ought to have done. He was not fifty yet, but he was beginning to look like an old man. The burden and heat of the day were telling on him sadly.

"Right, my Lord," replied the Prior; "yet let me beg of your Lordship not to overweary yourself. Your life is a precious thing to all dependent on you, and not less to us, your poor bedesmen here."

o

" Ah, Father ! is my life precious to any one ? " was the response, with a sad smile.

" Indeed it is," answered the Prior earnestly. " As your Lordship has just said, he who shall come after you may be harsh and unkind, and your poor serfs may sorely feel the change. No man has a right to throw away life, my Lord, and you have much left to live for."

Perhaps the Earl had grown a little morbid. Was it any wonder if he had ? He shook his head.

" We have but one life," continued the Prior, "and it is our duty to make the best of it—that is, to do God's will with it. And when it is God's will to say unto us, ' Come up higher,' we may be sorry that we have served Him no better, but not, I think, that we have given no more time to our own ease, nor even to our own sorrows."

" And yet," said the Earl, resting his head upon one hand, "one gets very, very tired sometimes of living."

" Cannot we trust our Father to call us to rest when we really need it ? " asked the Prior. " Nor is it well that in looking onward to the future glory we should miss the present rest to be had by coming to Him, and casting all our cares and burdens at His feet."

" Does He always take them ? "

" Always—if we give them. But there is such a thing as asking Him to take them, and holding them out to Him, and yet keeping fast hold of the other end ourselves. He will hardly take what we do not give."

The Earl looked earnestly into his friend's eyes.

"Father, I will confess that these seven years— nay! what am I saying? these eight-and-twenty— I have not been willing that God should do His will. I wanted my will done. For five-and-forty years, ever since I could lisp the words, I have been saying to Him with my lips, *Fiat voluntas tua.* But only within the last few days have I really said to Him in my heart, Lord, have Thy way. It seemed to me— will you think it very dreadful if I confess it?—that I wanted but one thing, and that it was very hard of God not to let me have it. I did not say such a thing in words; I could talk fluently of being resigned to His will, but down at the core of my heart I was resigned to everything but one, and I was not resigned to that at all. And I think I only became resigned when I gave over trying and working at resignation, and sank down, like a tired child, at my Father's feet. But now I am very tired, and I would fain that my Father would take me up in His arms."

The Prior did not speak. He could not. He only looked very sorrowfully into the worn face of the heart-wearied man, with a conviction which he was unable to repress, that the time of the call to come up higher was not far away. He would have been thankful to disprove his conclusion, but to stifle it he dared not.

"I hope," said the Earl in the same low tone, "that there are quiet corners in Heaven where weary men and women may lie down and rest a while at our Lord's feet. I feel unfit to take a place all at once in the angelic choir. Not unready to praise—I mean not that—only too weary, just at first, to care for anything but rest."

There were tears burning under the Prior's eyelids; but he was silent still. That was not his idea of Heaven; but then he was less weary of earth. He felt almost vexed that the only passage of Scripture which would come to him was one utterly unsuited to the occasion—"They rest not day nor night." Usually fluent and fervent, he was tongue-tied just then.

'Did Christ our Lord need the rest of His three days and nights in the grave?" suggested the Earl, thoughtfully. "He must have been very weary after the agony of His cross. I think He must have been very tired of His life altogether. For was it not one passion from Bethlehem to Calvary? And He could hardly have been one of those strong men who never seem to feel tired. Twice we are told that He was weary—when He sat on the well, and when He slept in the boat. Father, I ought to ask your pardon for speaking when I should listen, and seeming to teach where I ought to be taught."

"Nay, my Lord, say not so, I pray you." The Prior found his voice at last. "I have learned to recognise my Master's voice, whether I hear it from the rostrum of the orator or from the lowly hovel of the serf. And it is not the first time that I have heard it in yours."

The Earl looked up with an expression of surprise, and then shook his head again with a smile.

"Nay, good Father, flatter me not so far."

He might have added more, but the sound of an iron bar beaten on a wooden board announced the hour of supper. The Earl conversed almost cheerfully with the Prior and his head officers during supper; and Ademar remarked to the Cellarer that he had not for a long while seen his master so like his old self.

The first of October rose clear and bright. At Berkhamstead, the ladies were spending the morning in examining the contents of a pedlar's well-stocked pack, and buying silk, lawn, furs, and trimmings for the wedding. At Ashridge, the Earl was walking up and down the Priory garden, looking over the dilapidations which time had wrought in his monastery, and noting on his tables sundry items in respect of which he meant to repair the ravages. At Romsey, Mother Margaret, in her black patched habit and up-turned sleeves, was washing out the convent refectory, and thereby, she fervently hoped, washing her sins out of existence—without a thought of the chivalrous love which would have set her high above all such menial labour, and would never have permitted even the winds of heaven to "visit her cheek too roughly." Did it never occur to her that she might have allowed the Redeemer of men to "make her salvation" for her, and yet have allowed herself to make her husband's life something better to him than a weary burden?

The day's work was over, and the recreation time had come. The Prior of Ashridge tapped at the door of the guest-chamber, and was desired to enter.

He found the Earl turning over the leaves of his Psalter.

"Look here, Father," said the latter, pointing out the fifteenth verse of the ninetieth Psalm.

"We are glad for the days wherein Thou didst humiliate us; the years wherein we have seen evil."

"What does that mean?" said the Earl. "Is it that we thank God for the afflictions He has given us? It surely does not mean—I hope not—that our comfort is to last just as long as our afflictions have lasted, and not a day longer."

"Ah, my Lord, God is no grudging giver," answered the Prior. "The verse before it, methinks, will reply to your Lordship—'we exult and are glad all our days.' All our earthly life have we been afflicted; all our heavenly one shall we be made glad."

"Glad! I hardly know what the word means," was the pathetic reply.

"You will know it then," said the Prior.

"You will—but shall I? I have been such an unprofitable servant!"

"Nay, good my Lord, but are you going to win Heaven by your own works?" eagerly demanded the Bonus Homo. "'Beginning in the spirit, are ye consummated in the flesh?' Surely you have not so learned Christ. Hath He not said, 'Life eternal give I to them; and they shall not perish for ever, and none shall snatch them out of My hand'?"

"True," said the Earl, bowing his head.

But this was Vaudois teaching. And though Earl Edmund, first of all men in England, had drunk in the Vaudois doctrines, yet even in him they had to struggle with a mass of previous teaching which required to be unlearned—with all that rubbish of man's invention which Rome has built up on the One Foundation. It was hard, at times, to keep the old ghosts from coming back, and troubling by their shadowy presence the soul whom Christ had brought into His light.

There was silence for a time. The Earl's head was bent forward upon his clasped hands on the table, and the Prior, who thought that he might be praying, forbore to disturb him. At length he said, "My Lord, the supper-hour is come."

The Earl gave no answer, and the Prior thought he had dropped asleep. He waited till the board was struck with the iron bar as the signal for supper. Then he rose and addressed the Earl again. The silence distressed him now. He laid his hand upon his patron's shoulder, but there was no response. Gently, with a sudden and terrible fear, he lifted the bowed head and looked into his face. And then he knew that the weary heart was glad at last—that life eternal in His beatific presence had God given to him.

From far and near the physicians were summoned

that night, but only to tell the Prior what he already knew. They stood round the bed on which the corpse had been reverently laid, and talked of his mysterious disease in hard words of sonorous Latin. It would have been better had they called it in simple English what it was—a broken heart. Why such a fate was allotted to one of the best of all our princes, He knows who came to bind up the broken-hearted, and who said by the lips of His prophet, "Reproach hath broken mine heart."

Ademar was sent back to Berkhamsted with the woful news. There was bitter mourning there. It was not, perhaps, in many of the household, unmixed with selfish considerations, for to a large proportion of them the death of their master meant homelessness for the present, and to nearly all sad apprehensions for the future. Yet there was a great deal that was not selfish, for the gentle, loving, humane, self-abnegating spirit of the dead had made him very dear to all his dependants, and more hearts wept for him than he would ever have believed possible.

But there was one person in especial to whom it was felt the news ought to be sent. The Prior despatched no meaner member of the Order, but went himself to tell the dark tidings at Romsey.

He pleaded hard for a private interview with the Countess, but the reigning Abbess of Romsey was a great stickler for rule, and she decided that it was against precedent, and therefore propriety, that one of her nuns should be thus singled out from the rest.

The announcement must be made in the usual way, to the whole convent, at vespers.

So, in the well-known tones of the Prior of Ashridge,—some time the Earl's confessor, and his frequent visitor,—with the customary request to pray for the repose of the dead, to the ears of Mother Margaret, as she knelt in her stall with the rest, came the sound of the familiar name of Edmund, Earl of Cornwall.

Very tender and pathetic was the tone in which the intimation was given. The heart of the Prior himself was so wrung that he could not imagine such a feeling as indifference in that of the woman who had been the dearest thing earth held for that dead man. But if he looked down the long row of black, silent figures for any sign or sound, he looked in vain. There was not even a trembling of Mother Margaret's black veil as her voice rose untroubled in the response with all the rest,—

> " *O Jesu dulcis ! O Jesu pie!*
> *O Jesu, Fili Mariæ !*
> *Dona eis requiem.*"

In the recreation-time which followed, the Prior sought out Mother Margaret. He found her without difficulty, seated on a form at the side of the room, talking to a sister nun, and he caught a few words of the conversation as he approached.

" I assure thee, Sister Regina, it is quite a mistake. Mother Wymarca told me distinctly that the holy

Mother gave Sister Maud an unpatched habit, and
it is all nonsense in her to say there was a patch on
the elbow."

The Prior bit his lips, but he restrained himself,
and sat down, reverently saluted by both nuns as
he did so. Was she trying to hide her feelings?
thought he.

"Sister Margaret, I brought you tidings," he said,
as calmly as was in him.

The nun turned upon him a pair of cold, steel-blue
eyes, as calm and irresponsive as if he had brought
her no tidings whatever.

"I heard them, Father, if it please you. Has he
left any will ?"

The priest-nature in the Prior compelled him
officially to avoid any reprehension of this perfect
monastic calm ; but the human nature, which in his
case lay beneath it, was surprised and repelled.

"He has left a will, wherein you are fully provided for."

"Oh, that is nice !" said Mother Margaret, in tones
of unquestionable gratulation. "And how much am
I to have? Of course I care about it only for the
sake of the Abbey."

The Prior had his private ideas on that point; for,
as he well knew, the vow of poverty was somewhat
of a formality in the Middle Ages, since the nun
who brought to her convent a title and a fortune
was usually not treated in the same manner as a
penniless commoner.

" The customary dower to a widow, Sister."

" Do you mean to say I am only to have my third ?
Well, I call that shameful! And so fond of me as
he always professed to be! I thought he would
have left me everything."

The Prior experienced a curious sensation in his
right arm, which, had Mother Margaret not been a
woman, or had he been less of a Christian and a
Church dignitary, might have resulted in the measuring of her length on the floor of the recreation-
room. But she was totally unconscious of any such
feeling on his part. Her heart—or that within her
which did duty for one—had been touched at last.

" Well, I do call it disgraceful !" she repeated.

" And is that all ?" asked the Prior involuntarily,
and not by any means in consonance with his duty
as a holy priest addressing a veiled nun. But priests
and nuns have no business with hearts of any sort,
and he ought to have known this as well as she did.

" All ?" she said, with a rather puzzled look in the
frosty blue eyes. " I would it had been a larger sum,
Father; for the convent's sake, of course."

" And am I to hear no word of regret, Sister, for
the man to whom you were all the world ?"

This was, of course, a most shocking speech, considering the speaker and the person whom he addressed ; but it came warm from that inconvenient
heart which had no business to be beneath the Prior's
cassock. Mother Margaret was scandalised, and she
showed it in her face, which awoke her companion

to the fact that he was not speaking in character. That a professed nun should be expected to feel personal and unspiritual interest in an extern! and, as if that were not enough, in a man! Mother Margaret's sense of decorum was quite outraged.

"How could such thoughts trouble the blessed peace of a holy sister?" she wished to know. "Pardon me, Father; I shall pray for his soul, of course. What could I do more?"

And the Prior recognised at last that to the one treasure of that dead man's heart, the news he brought was less than it had been to him.

He bit his lips severely. It was all he could do to keep from telling her that the pure, meek, self-abnegating soul which had passed from earth demanded far fewer prayers than the cold, hard, selfish spirit which dwelt within her own black habit.

"It is I who require pardon, Sister," he said, in a constrained voice. "May our Lord in His mercy forgive us all!"

He made no further attempt to converse with Mother Margaret. But, as he passed her a few minutes later, he heard that she and Sister Regina had gone back to the previous subject, which they were discussing with some interest in their tones.

"O woman, woman!" groaned the Prior, in his heart; "the patch on Sister Maud's elbow is more to thee than all the love thou hast lost. Ah, my dear Lord! it is not you that I mourn. You are far better hence."

From which speech it will be seen that the Bonus Homo was very far from being a perfect monk.

The actions of Mother Margaret admirably matched her words. She gave herself heart and soul to the important business of securing her miserable third of her dead lord's lands and goods. Not till they were safe in her possession did she allow herself any rest.

Did the day ever come when her feelings changed? During the ten years which she outlived the man who had loved her with every fibre of his warm, great heart, did her heart ever turn regretfully, when Abbesses were harsh or life was miserable, to the thought of that tender, faithful love which, so far as in it lay, would have sheltered her life from every breath of discomfort? Did she ever in all those ten years whisper to herself,

> "Oh, if he would but come again,
> I think I'd vex him so no more!"

Did she ever murmur such words as,

> "I was not worthy of you, Douglas,
> Not half worthy the like of you!"

—words which, honestly sobbed forth in very truth, would have been far nearer real penitence than all the "acts of contrition" which passed her lips day by day.

God knoweth. Men will never know. But all history and experience tend to assure us that women such as Margaret de Clare usually die as they have lived, and that of all barriers to penitence and conversion there is none so hard to overthrow as indulged malice and deliberate hardening of the heart against the love of God and man.

There was not, as Piers and Clarice had feared there might have been, any misfortune to them in the way of preventing their marriage. King Edward had great respect for justice and honour, and finding that his cousin had, though without legal formalities, granted Clarice's marriage to Piers, he confirmed the grant, and Father Bevis married them quietly in the chapel of Berkhamsted Castle, without any festivity or rejoicings, for the embalmed body of the master to whom they owed so much lay in state in the banquet-hall. It was a mournful ceremony, where

> " The cheers that had erst made the welkin ring
> Were drowned in the tears that were shed for the King."

Clarice and Piers made no attempt to obtain any further promotion. They retired to a little estate in Derbyshire, which shortly afterwards fell to Piers, and there they spent their lives, in serving their generation according to the will of God, often brightened by visits from Ademar and Heliet, who had taken up their abode not far from them in the neighbouring county of Rutland. And as time went on, around Clarice grew up brave sons and fair daughters, to all of whom she made a very loving mother; but, perhaps, no one was ever quite so dear to her heart as the star which had gleamed on her life the brighter for the surrounding darkness, the little white rosebud which had been gathered for the garden of God.

> " In other springs her life might be
> In bannered bloom unfurled ;
> But never, never match her wee
> White Rose of all the world."

It was not until the spring which followed his death was blooming into green leaves and early flowers that the coffin of Edmund, Earl of Cornwall, was borne to the magnificent Abbey of Hales in Gloucestershire, founded by his father. There they laid him down by father and mother—the grand, generous, spendthrift Prince who had so nearly borne the proud title of Cæsar Augustus, and the fair, soft, characterless Princess who had been crowned with him as Queen of the Romans. For the Prince who was laid beside them that Easter afternoon, the world had prepared what it considers a splendid destiny. Throne and diadem, glory and wealth, love and happiness, were to have been his, so far as it lay in the world's power to give them ; but on most of all these God had laid His hand, and forbidden them to come near the soul which He had marked for His own. For him there was to be an incorruptible crown, but no corruptible ; the love of the Lord that bought him, but not the love of the woman on whom he set his heart. Now—whatever he may have thought on earth—now, standing on the sea of glass, and having the harp of God, he knows which was the better portion.

He wore no crown; he founded no dynasty; he passed away, like a name written in water, followed only by the personal love of a few hearts which were soon dust like him, and by the undying curses and calumnies of the Church which he had done his best to purify against her will.   But shall we, looking back across the six centuries which lie between us and him who brought Protestantism into England —shall we write on his gravestone in the ruined Abbey of Hales, "This man lived in vain"?

THE END.

Tales of English Life in the Olden Time.

By EMILY S. HOLT.

Large Cr. 8vo, FIVE SHILLINGS each.

THE HARVEST OF YESTERDAY.
A Tale of the Sixteenth Century.

COUNTESS MAUD ; or, The Changes of the World.
A Tale of the Fourteenth Century.
"Miss Holt's books are not only highly readable, but historical studies of much value."—*Spectator.*

MINSTER LOVEL. A Story of the Days of Laud.
"Capitally written, and enjoyable from first to last."—*The Scotsman.*

IT MIGHT HAVE BEEN. The Story of Gunpowder Plot.
"A well-constructed and well-told tale. We know of no one whose historical fiction is more trustworthy."—*Spectator.*

OUT IN THE '45; or, Duncan Keith's Vow.
"No one can fail to find pleasure in the quaint picturesque tale which Miss Holt sets forth."—*Spectator.*

IN CONVENT WALLS. The Story of the Despensers.
"The characters are carefully studied and vividly presented, while sound research is skilfully utilized in suggesting the life and colour of the historical period selected by the writer."—*Saturday Review.*

IN ALL TIME OF OUR TRIBULATION.
The Story of Piers Gaveston.
"A highly meritorious attempt to familiarize nineteenth century readers with the confusions of a long past century little known and less understood."—*Academy.*

THE LORD MAYOR. A Tale of London in 1384.
"Full of stirring incident graphically told."—*The Christian.*

LADY SYBIL'S CHOICE. A Tale of the Crusades.
"The book charms from the naïve simplicity of the heroine and from the skill with which the authoress has preserved the spirit of the age."—*The Graphic.*

WEARYHOLME ; or, Seedtime and Harvest.
"A skilful picture of the Restoration period."—*Graphic.*

A TANGLED WEB. A Tale of the Fifteenth Century.
"A charming book. . . . We heartily commend it."—*Sword and Trowel.*

RED AND WHITE. A Tale of the Wars of the Roses.
"A charming historical Tale, full of clever portraiture and antique colouring."
Publishers' Circular.

LONDON : JOHN F. SHAW & Co., 48, PATERNOSTER ROW, E.C.

STORIES BY LOUISE MARSTON.

MISS MOLLIE AND HER BOYS; or, His Great Love.
Large Crown 8vo, cloth, 3/6.

"The love of God is charmingly illustrated by a recital of the loving devotion of a young woman who bestowed affectionate care upon some poor lonely lads."
The Christian.

TWO LITTLE BOYS; or, I'd Like to Please Him.
Crown 8vo, cloth, Illustrated, 2/6.

' A wonderfully pathetic story. It will be read with deep feeling, especially by children, to whom the strikingly illustrated cover will prove an additional attraction."—*The Record.*

MR. BARTHOLOMEW'S LITTLE GIRL.
Crown 8vo, cloth, Illustrated, 2/6.

"A story that should turn the hearts of many to the Saviour. It is well written, and the teaching is pure and true."—*The Christian.*

CRIPPLE JESS. The Hop Picker's Daughter.
Crown 8vo, cloth, Illustrated, 2/6.

" Fully as engrossing as anything from the pen of Hesba Stretton."
The Christian.

"A sketch well drawn of a sweet flower blooming in a very humble place."
Woman's Work.

ROB AND MAG. A Little Light in a Dark Corner.
Crown 8vo, cloth, 1/6.

"A beautiful sketch."—*Churchman's Magazine.*

"We believe this little volume will be found the means of leading many to Jesus."—*The Christian.*

BLIND NETTIE; or, Seeking Her Fortune. 1/-

JITANA'S STORY; or, Light in the Darkness. 1/-

BENNIE, THE KING'S LITTLE SERVANT. 1/-

STORIES BY JENNIE CHAPPELL.

BERNE'S BARGAIN.
Large Crown 8vo, cloth, with Illustrations, 3/6.

"A delightful story. Boys cannot fail to like it. It is full of incident and adventure. The illustrations are excellent.'—*Manchester Examiner.*

FOR ELSIE'S SAKE; or, A Seaside Friendship.
Crown 8vo, cloth, Illustrated, 1/6.

LITTLE RADIANCE. A Year in a Child's Life.
Crown 8vo, cloth, Illustrated, 1/6.

"A charming book for children."—*Footsteps of Truth.*

HAND IN HAND; or, Radiance at Beechdale.
Crown 8vo, cloth, Illustrated, 1/6.

LEFT BEHIND; or, A Summer in Exile. Cloth, 1/-

OUGHTS AND CROSSES. A Story for Boy. 1/-

LONDON: JOHN F. SHAW & Co., 48, PATERNOSTER ROW, E.C.

STORIES BY E. EVERETT-GREEN.

SHADOWLAND ; or, What Lindie Accomplished.
Crown 8vo, with Illustrations, 1/6.
"A charming story for children, very prettily got up."—*Record.*

HER HUSBAND'S HOME ; or, The Durleys of Linley Castle.
Large Crown 8vo, cloth extra, with Illustrations, 3/6.
"Some of the scenes are particularly effective."—*Spectator.*

MARJORIE AND MURIEL ; or, Two London Homes.
Small 8vo, cloth extra, with Illustrations, 2/6.
"A capital story, very prettily got up."—*Record.*

HIS MOTHER'S BOOK. Crown 8vo, cloth extra, 2/-
"Little Bill is so lovable, and meets with such interesting friends, that everybody may read about him with pleasure."—*Spectator.*

LITTLE FREDDIE ; or, Friends in Need. Crown 8vo, cloth extra, 2/-
"There is real pathos in this story, telling how a poor little waif is protected from evil by the recollection of a lost mother's teaching."—*Liverpool Courier.*

BERTIE CLIFTON ; or, Paul's Little Schoolfellow.
Crown 8vo, cloth, 2/-
"Seldom have we perused a tale of the length of this with so much pleasure."
The Schoolmaster.

LITTLE RUTH'S LADY. Crown 8vo, with Illustrations, 2/-
"A delightful study of children, their joys and sorrows."—*Athenæum.*
"One of those children's stories that charm grown people as well as little folk."
Guardian.

OUR WINNIE ; or, When the Swallows Go.
Crown 8vo, cloth, Illustrated, 1/6.
"The beautiful life of little Winnie is one which all children will do well to take as an example."—*Banner.*

STORIES BY J. M. CONKLIN.

JUST AS IT OUGHT TO BE ; or, The Story of Miss Prudence.
Large Crown 8vo, cloth extra, 5/-
"Very original, interesting, with many good and suggestive thoughts."
"A capital book for girls."—*Baptist.*   *English Churchman.*

BEK'S FIRST CORNER, AND HOW SHE TURNED IT.
Large Crown 8vo, cloth, 3/6.
"Bek Westerley is a very charming person."—*Standard.*

OUT IN GOD'S WORLD ; or, Electa's Story. Large Crown 8vo, 3/6.
"One of the best girls' stories we have read."—*The Congregationalist.*

LONDON : JOHN F. SHAW & CO., 48, PATERNOSTER ROW, E.C.

STORIES BY L. T. MEADE.

Author of "*Scamp and I*," &o.

GREAT ST. BENEDICT'S; or, Dorothy's Story.

New and Cheaper Edition. Crown 8vo, cloth extra, with Illustrations, 3/6.

"The description of Dorothy's life is excellent."—*Spectator*.

"At once a noble book, and a most interesting story."—*Court Circular*.

A KNIGHT OF TO-DAY. A Tale.

New and Cheaper Edition. With Illustrations. Crown 8vo, cloth extra, 3/6.

"A finely-imagined story of a good man. It is a book well worth reading."
The Guardian.

BEL-MARJORY. A Tale. Crown 8vo, cloth extra, 6/-

"Most interesting; we give it our hearty commendation."—*English Independent*.

SCAMP AND I. A Story of City Byeways.

Crown 8vo, cloth extra, with Illustrations, 2/6.

"All as true to life and as touchingly set forth as any heart could desire.'
Athenæum.

THE CHILDREN'S KINGDOM;

Or, The Story of a Great Endeavour. Crown 8vo, cloth extra, with Illustrations, 3/6.

"A really well-written story, with many touching passages. Boys and girls will read it with eagerness and profit."— *The Churchman*.

WATER GIPSIES. A Tale.

Crown 8vo, cloth extra, with Illustrations, 2/6.

"It is full of incident from beginning to end, and we do not know the person who will not be interested in it."—*Christian World*.

DAVID'S LITTLE LAD.

Crown 8vo, cloth extra, with Illustrations, 2/6.

"A finely-imagined story, bringing out in grand relief the contrast between quiet, steady self-sacrifice, and brilliant, flashy qualities."—*Guardian*.

DOT AND HER TREASURES.

With Illustrations. Small 8vo, cloth extra, 2/-

"One of the tales of poor children in London, of which we have had many examples; but none finer, more pathetic, or more original than this."
Nonconformist.

OUTCAST ROBIN; or, Your Brother and Mine.

Illustrated. Small 8vo, cloth extra, 2/-.

WHITE LILIES, AND OTHER TALES.

With Illustrations. Small 8vo, cloth extra, 1/6.

"Stories of a singularly touching and beautiful character."—*Rock*.

LETTIE'S LAST HOME. Small 8vo, cloth extra, 1/6.

"Very touchingly told."—*Aunt Judy's Magazine*.

THOSE BOYS. A Story for all Little Fellows. Small 8vo, 1/-

LITTLE TROUBLE THE HOUSE. Small 8vo, 1/-

LONDON: JOHN F. SHAW & Co., 48, PATERNOSTER ROW, E.C.

STORIES BY CATHARINE SHAW.

Price Three Shillings and Sixpence each.

THE STRANGE HOUSE; or, A Moment's Mistake.

"A charming story. It is characterised by simplicity of treatment, but the interest is cleverly sustained, and the characters are well drawn."
Manchester Examiner.

LILIAN'S HOPE. Large Crown 8vo, cloth extra. With Illustrations.

"One of the best gift books for girls we have seen. The story throbs with the power and pathos of real home life."—*In His Name.*

DICKIE'S SECRET. Large Crown 8vo. Illustrated.

"We heartily welcome 'Dickie's Secret.' It is a delightful story."—*Record.*

DICKIE'S ATTIC. Large Crown 8vo.

"The prettiest story Mrs. Shaw has yet written."—*Standard.*
"A naturally pathetic subject treated with much skill as well as taste."
Spectator.

ON THE CLIFF; or, Alick's Neighbours. Large Crown 8vo.

"It is refreshing to come upon such a book as this, written with a clear, modest aim of revealing the beauty and happy privileges of the Christian life."
Church Sunday School Magazine.

FATHOMS DEEP; or, Courtenay's Choice. Large Crown 8vo.

"Not 'Fathoms Deep,' but on the surface, our Authoress has placed the life-giving Gospel. This is a capital book, and is cheap."—*Sword and Trowel.*

ALICK'S HERO. Large Crown 8vo, cloth. Illustrated.

"Mrs. Shaw has added to our delight in noble boyhood, as well as to her own reputation, in this most charming of her works."—*The Christian.*

HILDA; or, Seeketh Not Her Own. Crown 8vo, cloth extra.

"A charming story, illustrative of the blessedness of self-sacrifice."
Literary World.

Price Two Shillings and Sixpence each.

ONLY A COUSIN. Crown 8vo, cloth extra.

"In our excavations among heaps of tales we have not come upon a brighter jewel than this."—Rev. C. H. SPURGEON in *Sword and Trowel.*

THE GABLED FARM; or, Young Workers for the King. Crown 8vo, cloth extra.

"A charming story, wherein the children are described naturally."
Evangelical Magazine.

IN THE SUNLIGHT AND OUT OF IT. A Year of my Life-story. Crown 8vo, cloth extra.

"One of the pleasantest books that a girl could take into her hand, either for Sunday or week-day reading."—*Daily Review.*

NELLIE ARUNDEL. A Tale of Home Life. Crown 8vo, cloth extra, Illustrated.

"We need scarcely say that Mrs. Shaw holds out the light of life to all her readers, and we know of few better books than those which bear her name."
Record.

JACK FORESTER'S FATE. Crown 8vo, with Illustrations. 2/-

LONDON: JOHN F. SHAW & CO., 48, PATERNOSTER ROW, E.C.

POPULAR HOME STORIES.

By EMILY BRODIE.

OLD CHRISTIE'S CABIN. Crown 8vo, 2/6. Illustrated.
"A capital book for young people, depicting the loveliness of a ministering life on the part of some happy children."—*The Christian.*

COUSIN DORA; or, Serving the King. Large Crown 8vo, 2/6.
"An admirable tale for elder girls."—*Nonconformist.*

HIS GUARDIAN ANGEL. Large Crown 8vo, 3/6.
"Should find its way into school libraries as well as into homes."
Sunday School Chronicle.

FIVE MINUTES TOO LATE; or, Leslie Harcourt's Resolve.
Large Crown 8vo, cloth extra, 3/6.

NORMAN AND ELSIE; or, Two Little Prisoners.
Large Crown 8vo, extra cloth, 3/6.
"So true and delightful a picture that we can hardly believe we have only read about it; it all seems so real, and has done us so much good."—*The Christian.*

NORA CLINTON; or, Did I Do Right? Crown 8vo, 3/6.
"Will be read with pleasure and profit."—*Christian Age.*

LONELY JACK and His Friends at Sunnyside. Crown 8vo, 3/6.
"Its chapters will be eagerly devoured by the reader."—*Christian World.*

THE HAMILTONS; or, Dora's Choice. Crown 8vo, 3/6.
"Miss Brodie's stories have that savour of religious influence and teaching which makes them valuable as companions of the home."—*Congregationalist.*

UNCLE FRED'S SHILLING : Its Travels and Adventures.
Crown 8vo, cloth extra, 3/6.
"Children will follow it with as eager interest as the little people who listened to it in the book itself."—*Christian World.*

ELSIE GORDON ; or, Through Thorny Paths.
Crown 8vo, cloth extra, 2/6.
"The characters have been well thought out. We are sure the volume will be welcome at many a fireside."—*Daily Express.*

JEAN LINDSAY, the Vicar's Daughter. Crown 8vo, 2/6.
"The tale is admirably told, and some capital engravings interpret its principal incidents."—*Bookseller.*

ROUGH THE TERRIER. His Life and Adventures.
Illustrated by T. Pym. Square, cloth extra, 2/6; or boards, 1/6.
"A clever autobiography, cleverly illustrated."—*The Christian.*

SYBIL'S MESSAGE. Small 8vo, cloth extra, 1/6.

EAST AND WEST; or, The Strolling Artist. 1/6.

THE SEA GULL'S NEST; or, Charlie's Revenge. 1/6.

RUTH'S RESCUE; or, The Light of Ned's Home. 1/-

BOOKS FOR BOYS.

By M. L. RIDLEY.

Price Two Shillings and Sixpence each, with Illustrations.

SENT TO COVENTRY; or, The Boys of Highbeech.
Illustrated. Large Crown 8vo, cloth extra.
"A really good story of boys' school-life."—*Pall Mall Gazette.*
"Eminently interesting from start to finish."—*Pictorial World.*

KING'S SCHOLARS; or, Work and Play at Easthaven.
Illustrated. Large Crown 8vo, cloth extra.
"Full of all those stirring incidents which go to make up the approved life of schoolboys. Both adventure and sentiment find a place in it."—*Pall Mall Gazette.*
"A schoolboy tale of very good tone and spirit."—*Guardian.*

OUR CAPTAIN. The Heroes of Barton School.
With Illustrations. Crown 8vo, cloth extra.
"A first-class book for boys."—*Daily Review.*
"A regular boy's book."—*Christian World.*

THE THREE CHUMS. A Story of School Life.
With Illustrations. Crown 8vo, cloth extra.
"A book after a boy's heart. How can we better commend it than by saying it is both manly and godly?"—Rev. C. H. SPURGEON in *Sword and Trowel.*
"Ingeniously worked out and spiritedly told."—*Guardian.*

HILLSIDE FARM; or, Marjorie's Magic.
Crown 8vo. Illustrated.
"A very well-written story which all girls will thoroughly enjoy."—*Guardian.*

GOLDENGATES; or, Rex Mortimer's Friend. Large Crown 8vo.
"An excellent story of boyish love."—*Sunday School Chronicle.*
"A first-rate story for boys. The hero is a fine specimen of a manly young Christian."—*Congregational Review.*

OUR SOLDIER HERO. The Story of My Brothers.
Large Crown 8vo, cloth extra. With Illustrations.
"Contains the healthiest of matter presented in the most entertaining of ways."
Schoolmaster.
"An autobiography very simply and pleasantly written."—*Times.*

WALTER ALISON: His Friends and Foes.
Crown 8vo, cloth extra. With Illustrations.
"Schoolboys are sure to like it."—*Churchman.*
"A book boys will be sure to read if they get the chance."—*Sword and Trowel.*

LONDON: JOHN F. SHAW & CO., 48, PATERNOSTER ROW, E.C.

STORIES BY GRACE STEBBING.

LONDON: JOHN F. SHAW & Co., 48, PATERNOSTER ROW, E.C.

SPLENDID STORIES
FOR BOYS.

By DR. GORDON STABLES, R.N.

HEARTS OF OAK. A Story of Nelson and the Navy.
Large Crown 8vo, with Illustrations, 5/-

TWO SAILOR LADS.

A Story of Stirring Adventures on Sea and Land. Large Crown 8vo, cloth, with Illustrations, price 5/-

"A sea story, big with wonders."—*Saturday Review.*

"A capital story in Dr. Stables' best style."—*Spectator.*

FOR ENGLAND, HOME, AND BEAUTY.

A Tale of Battle and the Breeze. Large Crown 8vo, cloth, with Illustrations, price 5/-

"Dr. Stables has almost surpassed himself in this book. Certainly we have read nothing of his which has pleased us more—perhaps we might say, as much."
The Spectator.

EXILES OF FORTUNE.

The Story of a Far North Land. Large Crown 8vo, cloth extra, with Illustrations price 5/-

"A capital book; written with this popular writer's accustomed spirit, and sure to be enjoyed."—*Scotsman.*

"Boys of all growths will relish this story."—*Manchester Examiner.*

FROM SQUIRE TO SQUATTER.

A Tale of the Old Land and the New. Large Crown 8vo, Illustrated, price 5/-

"Just the sort of book that boys delight in, as the story is crowded with exciting incidents."—*Schoolmaster.*

"The story is naturally and brightly written, and shows a marked advance over former productions by the same author."—*Standard.*

IN THE DASHING DAYS OF OLD; or, The World-wide Adventures of Willie Grant. Large Crown 8vo, Illustrated, price 5/-

"We can commend this book as the best story for boys which we have read for many a day."—*English Churchman.*

"Can be safely recommended as one of the very best books that could possibly be placed in a boy's hand."—*Schoolmaster.*

By LADY FLORENCE DIXIE.

THE YOUNG CASTAWAYS; or, The Child Hunters of Patagonia.
Large Crown 8vo, cloth, with Illustrations, price 5/-

"A lively story of adventure, drawn a good deal from personal experience."
The Guardian.

LONDON: JOHN F. SHAW & Co., 48, PATERNOSTER ROW, E.C.

Tales of English Life in the Olden Time.

By EMILY S. HOLT.

ALL'S WELL; or, Alice's Victory.
With Illustrations. Large Crown 8vo. 3/6.

THE WHITE LADY OF HAZELWOOD. Large Crown 8vo. 3/6.
"An entertaining book of the instructive type, which we always take a special pleasure in commending."—*The Christian.*

BEHIND THE VEIL. A Story of the Norman Conquest. 3/6.
"Interesting from first to last."—*British Weekly.*

THE KING'S DAUGHTERS; or, How Two Girls kept the Faith.
Large Crown 8vo. Illustrated. 3/6.
"We never met with a book more suited to read aloud to young people on a Sunday afternoon."—*Record.*

YE OLDEN TIME. English Customs in the Middle Ages. 3/6.
"We have seldom met with a more useful book."—*Notes and Queries.*

MISTRESS MARGERY. A Tale of the Lollards. Crown 8vo, 2/6.
"A page in history which our young men and maidens will do well to saturate with holy tears."—*Sword and Trowel.*

JOHN DE WYCLIFFE. The First of the Reformers.
And What He Did for England. Crown 8vo, cloth extra, 3/6.
"An admirable exposition of the opinions of a remarkable man."
Notes and Queries.

A FORGOTTEN HERO; or, Not for Him.
The Story of Edmund Earl, of Cornwall. Crown 8vo, 3/6.
"We trust many will become acquainted with Miss Holt's 'Forgotten Hero.'"
The Christian.

THE MAIDEN'S LODGE; or, None of Self, and all of Thee.
A Tale of the Reign of Queen Anne. Crown 8vo, cloth extra, 2/6.

AT YE GRENE GRIFFIN. A Tale of the Fifteenth Century.
Small 8vo, cloth extra, 2/6.

THE WELL IN THE DESERT.
An Old Legend. Small 8vo, cloth extra, 2/-

FOR THE MASTER'S SAKE. Small 8vo, cloth extra, 2/-
"We heartily recommend this well-written tale."—*Churchman.*

OUR LITTLE LADY; or, Six Hundred Years Ago. 2/-
"A charming chronicle of the olden time."—*The Christian.*

THE WAY OF THE CROSS. A Tale of the Early Church. 1/6.

THE SLAVE GIRL OF POMPEII. With Illustrations. Cloth extra, 1/6.

ALL FOR THE BEST; or, Bernard Gilpin's Motto. 1/-

www.ingramcontent.com/pod-product-compliance
Lightning Source LLC
Chambersburg PA
CBHW020107030726
47498CB00006B/1990